JESSICA WATKINS PRESENTS

DESIGNER
Desires

KASEY MARTIN

D1506305

ISBN-13: 978-1517754495
ISBN-10: 1517754496

ACKNOWLEDGEMENTS

I would like to say thank you to my husband for being a constant supporter of my dreams, and to my mom for not hiding her romance novels well enough for me not to find them and read them as a kid.

I would also like to thank my friends and family for their love and encouragement,
and God for all his blessings.

"May I help you?" Korrine asked closing the door to just a crack.

"Why, yes, you absolutely can," the woman replied with an evil grin spreading across her face.

Korrine didn't like the look on the woman's face or in her eyes. She didn't recognize the leggy blond with the too tight dress. But the woman seemed to be familiar with her, and Korrine didn't like that feeling at all.

She moved to shut the door all the way when the woman caught Korrine off guard and shoved the door, knocking Korrine off balance while quickly moving inside.

The woman pulled a gun as her evil smile grew wider. Gasping, Korrine took a step back shaking her head at the woman. "Who-who are you?! What do you want?!" Korrine asked growing frantic.

The woman let out a maniacal laugh that showed she was clearly disturbed before dropping her handbag on the floor while wiping at the invisible lint on her short bandage dress.

"Oh, we aren't so tough, are we 'sweetness'? I overestimated you. Since you are from South Dallas, I just knew I would have to 'scrap' a little."

Korrine narrowed her eyes at the woman's blatant bigotry. "I don't know what you want, but you can take it and leave," she hissed through bated breath.

"Oh, I'm going to do just that and more, Korrine. I'm Misty, by the way. We haven't been introduced since Tony has been hiding you away. You see, I've been seeing Tony for quite some time, and I was planning on marrying him. We have a lot in common, he and I. Our families go way back, but he seems to have gotten distracted and strayed from my plans of matrimony. I tried to get him to see that you weren't on his level. A man of his caliber needs someone with a name and standing in the community. Tony needs me, and I need him. You don't have the pedigree that I have." Misty said this as if it was the sanest explanation in the world.

Korrine looked at the woman with a wide-eyed expression. Misty was rambling on as if Korrine should know what the hell she was ranting about.

"Misty, is it?" Korrine asked hesitantly. "Look, Tony and I aren't even dating anymore. We weren't even anything official. So I really don't know why you are in my house holding me at gunpoint. None of this makes any sense to me."

With her hands in the air, Korrine backed away stumbling over an end table by the door, knocking over a lamp. The sound of the lamp crashing to the floor made both women jump. Misty's hand shook slightly, giving away her true demeanor. She may have seemed calm, but the look in her eyes was pure insanity.

Korrine knew she had to stall this crazy person. Tony was on his way and would be there any moment. All she had to do was keep this heffa talking, and then she would be free from this deranged bitch.

"I really don't know what's going on or why you are here. Tony never mentioned he was getting married or even thinking about marriage. That's not something we talked about."

Misty gave another high-pitched laugh. "You aren't really that smart, are you? I don't have time to explain anything to you right now. So *you* look, Tony is probably on his way. I know the goons he has watching this place will be back from their shift change at any moment, so we need to get out of here."

Goons? Tony has someone watching my place? Why didn't he tell me? Obviously the threat was more serious than I thought since this crazy bitch is here with a gun. How does she know Tony is on his way? Korrine's thoughts were all over the place. The questions were popping in her head so fast that she didn't realize that Misty was about to slap her.

Whack!

Misty's hand came hard across Korrine's face, making her stumble back once again. "I said let's move, bitch! Don't just stand there daydreaming! I don't have time for this shit!"

Korrine stumbled back but didn't fall. She caught herself, seething with anger. *This bitch thinks she's bad with a gun. But if it's the last thing I do, I'm going to knock her the fuck out!* Korrine gathered her composure and narrowed her eyes at Misty before slowly moving toward the door. Once at the door, Korrine whirled around trying to catch Misty off guard, pushing her with all the strength she could muster. But Misty was watching closely and saw the move coming. Misty side stepped her and, although Korrine was able to knock her slightly off balance, Misty didn't lose her grip on the gun.

She smirked at Korrine and pushed her in the back. "Tsk tsk, 'sweetness.' That wasn't so sweet. You better be glad I still need to get you out of here, or I would put a bullet in your pretty little head. Now move, and don't try anything else or, so help me, I will find another way to get *your body* out of this shithole you call an apartment."

FOUR MOUTHS EARLIER...

CHAPTER 1

Korrine

He slowly slid his hands down the front of her body. He lightly touched her tender breasts, just enough to make her gasp. He chuckled, a low, rich sound that made her shudder. He smiled and continued the butterfly touches around her nipples, which now pebbled under his ministrations.

"Damn, baby, you feel so good…I can't get enough of you," came the deep baritone voice.

"Mmmm, baby…*Yes*," Korrine moaned with pleasure.

"Lift those legs around me, baby. I want to taste you."

Korrine lifted her legs and placed them around his muscular shoulders. He dipped his head, slowly kissing her calf all the way to her inner thigh. He began to caress her with his tongue, making lazy circles over her sensitive skin. He sucked and licked all the way to her core. Korrine's inner muscles started to clench….

BEEP! BEEP! BEEP! BEEP!

The annoying hammering of her alarm clock jolted Korrine out of her sleep. "SHIT!" As she fought to silence the alarm, she fussed. "Damn! That's the most action I've seen in a minute, and it had to be a dream. UUUGGGGH!!! Guess it's time to get up and finish this new design."

With a huff, Korrine stormed out of bed.

Korrine "Korri" Taylor was an up and coming designer. She knew she was destined to be in fashion. As a little girl she used to watch as her mother would get dressed, how she would coordinate her outfits, and sometimes even make her own dresses when she had the time. Korrine started to sneak swatches from her mother's sewing room to make different outfits for her dolls. She loved creating whimsical designs. Now, that was the main reason she was highly sought after by young starlets, socialites, and fashionistas. Korrine's designs had an appeal that was both youthful and sophisticated. Her work had intricate details that would sometimes take her weeks to hand sew. However, lately, she had enough orders to be able to outsource some of the more tedious sewing.

She started in her apartment, sketching and sewing her designs by herself. Now she had her very own studio that she was making and selling her clothes out of. The space was located in a warehouse district in Addison, TX. Although small, Korrine loved the location, as well as the space itself.

She worked hard to get where she was, and she was proud of all that she accomplished so far.

Korri was in the middle of putting the finishing touches on a one of a kind creation for a popular socialite's twenty-eighth birthday bash. This particular socialite just happened to also be Korri's close friend. If she played her cards right, her dress would be all over fashion blogs and gossip sites for weeks to come. The dress had to be right, it had to make a statement, and it had to be perfect.

****

"I absolutely love this dress, Korri!" Lauryn Cameron squealed as she twirled around like a five-year-old. Her excitement was infectious, and Korri couldn't help but smile along with the easy going fashionista. Korri met Lauryn at a runway show for an elite boutique over a year before. The two hit it off immediately and became fast friends.

Lauryn could make any outfit that she wore look like high-fashion. She had the perfect shape at 5'7" with long, tan legs, a nice shapely behind, and perky "girls" to top it off. Korrine loved to dress her. Lauryn could've easily been a model, but she would rather gallivant around the globe partying and spending her family's money than actually having a schedule to keep.

"So, Ms. Korrine Taylor, what will *you* be wearing to my oh-so-special birthday?"

"Uh…well…um…," Korrine stumbled. "I'm not sure yet, Lauryn."

"Come on, Korri, you have to look great for my big day-"

Korrine cut Lauryn off mid-sentence. "Lo, it's your birthday, not your wedding. And *I* don't have to look great…I just need to make sure *you* do!"

"Oh Korri," Lauryn sighed in exasperation. "You are one of my besties. Not only that, but you are one of the most beautiful people I know. You indeed have to be just as *fly* as me because, my dear, you will be photographed to the heavens when the press finds out that you are the fabulous designer of this equally fabulous frock."

Korri rolled her eyes. "Since when do you say the word *fly*, Lo?"

"Since I've been hanging with such *fly* people," Lauryn said with a cheeky smile and a wink.

Brandon, Korrine thought with a smile of her own. Brandon was one of Korrine's best friends, and one of his favorite words was "fly." That was mostly because he was one of the "flyest" people she knew.

"Look, Korri, I know that dressing other people is your thing. But I want you to make a little extra effort...for me...pleeeeaaaase?" Lauren whined, bringing Korrine's thoughts back to the present.

"Why does it matter what I look like, Lo? I don't need to be the center of anyone's attention."

"Well, you remember my cousin, Tony, right?" Lauryn rushed to get out.

"Sure. What does that have to do wi-" Korrine stopped mid-sentence. "Wait. What did you do, Lo?"

"Nothing, I promise." Yet, Lo's guilty expression said completely different.

"Lo!?"

"Okay, look, I might've mentioned that you were making my dress, and Tony remembers you. And he just asked if, and I quote, 'My little sexy designer friend would be at my party.'"

"Oh, geez, Lo! Why do you insist on fixing me up? I'm okay with being single," Korri said, clearly annoyed by her friend's meddling.

"Nobody is *okay* with being single, Korri. You're just complacent. It's time to get you out of this rut and back on the horse. I just want you to have a little fun. All work and no hump makes Korri a dull girl," Lauryn said with a smirk.

"Excuse me, but how do you know I haven't had a little hump now and then? And who in the hell said I wasn't fun? I'm fun!"

"Okay, okay! So let's *just say* you're fun. When was the last time you went on a date, had a kiss, or just a romp in the sack?"

Korri narrowed her eyes at her friend. "It's been a while, I have to admit. However, I've been busy. I'm trying to be a *boss*. I don't have time for 'romps in the sack,' as you so eloquently put it."

"Okay, so you don't have to have any romps. But a date now and then could loosen you up. Besides, Tony is the type of fun you need. And you can still be a boss...just a boss that's getting a little bit," Lauryn responded with a smile.

Korri let out a long sigh. "I'm not making any promises, Lo; I will put in a little extra effort...but...I'm not saying I'm dating anyone. You got me, fly girl?"

"I got you!" Lauryn beamed at Korri before sauntering off.

Korrine was still reeling from the mere mention of Lauryn's cousin, Tony. Antonio Cameron was sex on a stick...a pure unadulterated hunk of a man. At 6'5", he was built like a tank with strong everything. The man was H.O.T. He had naturally tan skin so smooth that Korrine lost her breath just thinking about how she could lick him from head to toe and back again. He had strong facial features, a sharp nose, and a chiseled jaw, but it was his piercing brown eyes and dimpled smile that could do you in.

Korrine didn't necessarily date white men, but Tony was just *so fine*. Who cared what color he was?

However, he was also arrogant and self-centered.

Korrine thought, "*No... one arrogant asshole was enough for a lifetime...Thanks.*

CHAPTER 2

Korrine

It had been four days since the conversation with Lauryn, and Korrine couldn't keep her mind from going over what Lo said. What the hell did she agree to? Korri couldn't help but think back to the last date she had, and she couldn't even remember the poor guy's name. *Am I really turning into a workaholic?* Korri thought to herself. It couldn't be that bad to have a date now and then, and to clear the bats out of the belfry would be a bonus. Plus Korrine kept having these erotic dreams; it had to be a reason for that, after all. Maybe, if she had a little action, she could stop being so distracted and actually get a good night's sleep.

Her last serious relationship was almost two years ago. Korrine was single by choice, though. She had plenty of offers from the opposite sex. Korrine always thought she was short at only 5'5," but she had a body to die for. She had track star legs that led up to a nice firm round backside. She had C-cup breasts and a small waist, but it was her face that could stop traffic. Korri had dark brown skin with a smooth, flawless complexion that covered plump bow lips and high cheek bones. But it was her eyes that would draw you in; they were hazel with flecks of green and slightly slanted, but still gave her a look of doe-eyed innocence. They were simply mesmerizing.

But it had been two years since Korrine's heart got broken, and she'd thrown herself into her work ever since. She dated occasionally when her friends set her up, but she hadn't had sex since her ex-fiancé, Darren.

Darren Franklin was the epitome of tall, dark, and handsome. He was 6'0" with caramel colored skin, dark brown eyes, and a swagger that couldn't be denied. He held attention whenever he entered a room. He was also charismatic to a fault and completely full of shit.

Korrine met Darren at the city's courthouse. She was taking care of a speeding ticket, and he was meeting a client. Darren was a hot defense attorney; he worked for one of the biggest law firms in Dallas. Korrine was completely captivated by his striking good looks and charm. He said all the right things...but, of course, he did...he was a lawyer, after all. Korrine wasn't naïve by any measure. She was an intelligent, independent woman, but her mother always told her to look out for snakes that were disguised as men.

Darren was just in the right place at the right time and saying all of the right things. She didn't need a man, but she wanted one at the time. He wined and dined Korrine, taking her to all of the hottest restaurants and events around the Dallas/Fort Worth area, or the DFW, as it's so often called. Korrine was never big on celebrities or status, but she couldn't help but be a little star struck when he had VIP and backstage access to all the concerts and parties in town. Darren introduced her to everyone everywhere they went. He was always telling her how beautiful she was and how she didn't have to work as long as she was "his girl."

Yet, Korrine and Darren began to often have arguments about her long work hours. He frequently said she cared more about her work than him, which was completely false. She always put him first above everything, even her career. Family was important to Korrine, especially since she didn't have much, and the man she loved was considered family. She cut back on work, designing less and less to spend more time with Darren. She made sure she was at his place making dinner every weeknight that he was home early. She was spending less time at her studio and her own apartment so she could essentially be at his beck and call. However, Darren wasn't satisfied with her simply cutting back; he wanted her to stop designing all together.

She lost herself in him, and yet it still wasn't enough. Korrine became increasingly unhappy with her love life, and, since she wasn't being creative, she was becoming unhappy with her work life as well. Compliments from Darren came sporadically and the insults more frequently. He stopped taking her out and started working later and later.

One day Korrine had enough. She went to Darren's high-rise condo in downtown Dallas to confront him about his behavior. When she used her key to get in, what Korrine was confronted with was Darren getting a blowjob from some skank.

"What- The- Fuck?!" Korrine shouted as she entered the swanky condo.

"Oh shit, baby! I was uh...." Darren paused as he tried pushing the bottle blonde off of his dick.

"You were uh...what? You asshole! I knew you were cheating, but my dumbass wanted to give you a chance. I wanted to come here and talk to you about our problems. But you know what? You can keep all the talking, arguing, and begging! I'm completely done with your black ass!"

"Korrine, wait. Baby..." There was a long pause, and then a sudden look of complete and utter superiority crossed Darren's face. Darren began with a sneer. "You know what? I'm glad you came when you did. Now I don't have to keep pretending to be in love with you. I'm a successful black man with money to burn, no kids, no baby mamas- nothing! You act like I'm not doing you a favor by being with you. Any woman would be lucky to have me. I'm too young to just settle for any old chick! You could've been set for life with me. Being my girl was a blessing!"

Korrine looked at Darren and really saw him for the first time. She began to laugh at the foolishness that she had let go on for so long. Once she regained control of her laughter, she looked at Darren again. His superior look had been replaced with shock and annoyance at Korrine's reaction.

"Boy, bye!" she chuckled. "First off, your ass is thirty-seven years old, so you're not that young. Second of all, you don't have money to burn. Just because you're burning money doesn't mean your ass ain't in debt. You can barely afford the rent on this place. Without the help of mommy dearest, you would be on the street in a New York minute...and you know it!"

Korrine turned to walk out when Darren grabbed her arm and shouted, "Fuck you, bit-"

Before he could get the word out, Korrine jerked her arm away, reared back, and slapped Darren with all the strength she had.

"Don't you ever put your hands on me! Who the hell do you think you are?! Have you lost your ever-loving mind? I'm done with you and this foolishness!"

Darren stumbled back, shocked from the slap. Korrine threw the keys at the blonde, who was now standing a few feet behind Darren with her mouth hanging open and stormed out of the condo...slamming the door in her wake. Later that night when Korrine was finally home and calm, she cried herself to sleep. Then and there she made a promise to herself to never again let another man put her in that position.

Korrine's phone started to vibrate, bringing her out of her daydream. She hated thinking about Darren. It took her to a dark place, a place where she relied too much on a man's approval. But she couldn't think about that right now. She had other things she needed to do.

Korrine sighed and picked up her vibrating phone.

"Hello."

"Hey, fly girl. What's up?"

"Hey, B. Not much. I'm just sitting here thinking about things, but what I really need to do is figure out what I'll be wearing to Lo's big day," Korrine said to her best friend, Brandon.

He laughed, "Oh Lord, you're not calling it her big day too, are you?"

"I know, I know," Korrine laughed.

"You sound like something's bothering you, chica. Want to meet up for a drink and tell big daddy what's wrong?"

"Uh...since when does anybody, let alone me, call you big daddy?" Korrine responded.

"I thought I would try it out; I need a new nickname," Brandon chuckled.

"You will always be 'B' to me. How about we meet in an hour at the spot?" Korrine said with a smile.

"Gloria's on Greenville?" Brandon responded.

"You know it!" Korrine beamed.

Korrine was practically floating on the way to Gloria's. She was jamming to her favorite radio station, *The Boom*, and she was virtually having her very own concert.

"Heard it all befoooore! All of ya lies! All of ya sweet talk! Baby this! Baby that! But ya lies ain't workin' now!"

Sunshine Anderson was the 'ish and after singing one of her jams in the loudest voice she could muster, Korrine was in a much better mood. Now that she was on her way to see her oldest friend, Brandon, things were really starting to look up.

Korrine and Brandon had been friends since their freshman year in high school. Korrine was the girl that was everybody's friend. She didn't do the cliques that high school was famous for. She just mixed in with everyone; easily blending in, but never standing out, unlike Brandon. He was the outspoken, outgoing, most popular, outstanding jock, drama geek, band nerd, and all around classic American boy. The girls loved him, with his low cut waves, smooth mocha colored skin, and deep brown eyes that looked almost black. Girls were so jealous of the fact that Korrine was the only girl he was ever really affectionate with. Brandon didn't bat an eye at their advances. He would take it all in stride, never showing any hints that he was living his life in the closet. He didn't come out of said closet until their sophomore year in college. Nobody ever had a clue, with the exception of Korrine. She always knew, and she never judged him. Brandon was her chosen family, and she would love him no matter what.

Once Korrine arrived at Gloria's, she immediately spotted Brandon sitting at their favorite table flirting with the obliviously straight male waiter.

"Brandon," Korri greeted with an admonishing tone.

"Korrine," Brandon said with a smirk.

Korrine sat down, and they ordered their favorite Spicy Mango Margaritas. Once the blushing waiter finished taking their drink orders and was out of earshot, both friends started to laugh.

"Now you know that boy is straight! Why are you flirting so hard?" Korrine said with a giggle.

"Oh, you know I like a challenge." Brandon smiled wickedly. "Besides, I wasn't flirting. I was just teasing him. We used to workout at the same gym. He knows I was only kidding around with him."

Korrine just shook her head at Brandon's antics.

"Anyways, when I called you earlier, you were upset. What's going on with you?" Brandon asked Korrine concerned.

"Well, Lo had me thinking. She's trying to fix me up with her cousin, Tony, and you know I don't need a man in my life right now, Korrine said exasperatedly.

"Why the hell not?!" Brandon replied. "And Tony is fine as hell!!"

"Fine or not, you know he is self-centered and you of all people know I don't do well with self-absorbed men!" Korrine practically yelled.

"Calm down, babygirl. You're getting all worked up for no reason," Brandon said in a serious tone. "Tony may be a little ...Uh... How can I say this? ... *Self-aware*. That's it! Tony may be a little self-aware, but not every guy is Darren, Korrine. You need to get over that shit already. Plus, nobody said you had to marry Tony. Just loosen up and have a little fun."

Korrine knew what he was saying was right. She definitely needed to get over what Darren did, but she just didn't want to be hurt again.

"I know. I will try to have more fun," Korrine replied with a small smile.

"Well, okay then! Let's drink and be merry. There's plenty of time to cry over men, and today is *not* that day. So cheers!" Brandon said.

Both Brandon and Korrine raised their glasses simultaneously to Brandon's suggestion.

****

After their drinks and laughter, Korrine and Brandon agreed that he would come over to her place and get ready for Lo's birthday party the next day. As per usual, they would go to the party together.

Well, at least I will have a date…even if it is Brandon.

Korrine was feeling somewhat better, and her non-love life would just have to take a backseat. But she couldn't shake the thought of potentially having to look at Antonio Cameron all night long. Who was she kidding? She would be more than happy to look, stare, touch, lick, and do anything else to Antonio Cameron. Alas, it wasn't meant to be. Tony was not the type of man a woman like Korrine needed; he was what Korri called a "man-whore." He had a different woman on his arm every time Korri laid eyes on him, but that didn't stop Tony from openly flirting with her every chance he got. The audacity of some men! He was so arrogant; but damn, he was fine!

CHAPTER 3

Korrine

Lauryn's party was that night, and Korrine still hadn't gotten Tony off her mind. Could he be the answer to her drought? Or was he just another distraction? Korri was clearly already distracted by the mere thought of Tony, so what would the actual man cause her? Korrine was ready for the thoughts of Tony to be done with. She was going to wear a sexy dress, and, for once in her life, she was going to let loose.

Thoughts of work and the pressure of success will have to take a backseat because tonight Korrine was going to show both Lauryn and Brandon that she could indeed have some fun!

Brandon would be over in an hour to help Korri with her hair and makeup. Korrine decided to wear a red dress with a lace overlay. It was a halter top design with just enough cleavage, and it had hem length that hit right above the knee. But the back was the show stopper. The dress dipped so low that it came to the end of her spine, right above the curve of her behind. It was sexy indeed, and Korri was definitely going to be *fly* tonight.

Brandon was right on time. Korri, however, was nowhere near ready.

"Korri, why aren't you ready? You know I hate to be late!" Brandon fussed with a frustrated moan.

"B, you have to help me!" Korri was frantically running around her uptown apartment looking for her shoes. She had the perfect pair of red bottoms that she splurged on to compliment her red dress that she couldn't find.

"Korri, just relax. Take deep breaths. You know I gotcha," Brandon replied shaking his head. "You're already wearing a fantastic dress, so all I have to do is something with that mess on top of your head. By the way...What-In-The-Hell?"

Korrine grimaced. "I know, I know...Just help me, please."

"All right, I'm going to get you a glass of wine so you can relax, *and* so I can put my magic to work without you fidgeting all over the place."

After another hour, Korrine was pulled, plucked, tucked, and prepped for the party. Brandon had undeniably worked his magic, and Korri was looking breathtakingly beautiful. Korrine couldn't get over how great she looked. Brandon had played up her hazel eyes with a smoky eye look and fake lashes. Korri had a smooth complexion, so she didn't need much foundation. He played up her kissable lips with a red matte lipstick and brushed her high cheekbones with a light pink blush. He styled her hair bone straight with a part down the middle. Her jet black hair hung to her shoulders in a sophisticated style.

"Damn, I'm good!" Brandon said with a satisfied smile.

Korrine looked at herself in the mirror. "HOLY SHITBALLS!" Korrine gasped. "Is that me?"

Brandon chuckled. "Shitballs? You've been hanging with Lo too much. Okay, baby girl, throw on those stilts you call shoes, and let's go shake some booty…and maybe even catch you a little piece, if you get my drift."

"Oh, I get your drift. I'm going to let loose and have a good time, but I'm not looking for anything."

"Well, my dear sweet Korrine, that's the best time to find a little somethin' somethin," Brandon smirked.

"When is that exactly?" Korrine sighed.

"When you're not looking!" Brandon replied with a wink.

****

The party looked amazing. Lauryn, of course, had a red carpet full of paparazzi and fashion bloggers. Korrine's design was a big hit. She had been anxious all night wondering about how her design would be perceived. She also had interviews to do with some of the top fashion bloggers. She was excited to get her name and designs out there, but she hated doing interviews; she felt tongue-tied and like she was saying the wrong things. However, Korrine knew that it was part of the process and she would do what she had to do to be a success. After all the paps took pictures of her, just like Lauryn said they would, and her interviews were complete, she went in search of the open bar or a waiter...whichever she came across first. She was in dire need of a drink. Now that the party was underway, she could finally relax and let loose.

Korri knew that Lauryn and Brandon were in the VIP section, so she headed to find that drink. There were throngs and throngs of partiers, but she didn't care. Korrine was determined to get a rum and coke or maybe even a shot if it killed her. The VIP section was on the other side of the club so, instead of trying to make it there, where the free drinks were, she decided that she would head towards the bar that was closest to her. Korrine wanted to stay true to her word and get loose, so instead of a rum and coke, she took two shots of tequila that went straight to her head. Then she headed to the dance floor to dance the night away. She forgot, for once, about the endless pressure she put herself under to be a success.

Korrine was happily dancing by herself when a stranger walked up behind her and started to grind against her backside. Korri stepped away but kept dancing. The stranger, however, did not take the hint and tried to grab Korri around her waist.

Korrine tried to smile to soften her rejection. "Whoa, big boy, I don't know you like that."

"Hey, baby, you're a fine piece of ass. I was just trying to give you a little play…no sense in a hot little number like you dancing by yourself," the stranger replied.

"I'm fine with dancing by myself, thanks." Korrine frowned looking around for Brandon or Lo.

The stranger ignored her and kept advancing forward.

"Look, baby, I'm just trying to show you a good time. Stop being such a stuck up little bitch," the stranger huffed.

Korrine sucked in a breath, trying to rein in her temper. She wasn't a hothead, but being called a bitch was one of her triggers. This bastard was trying her. She was a successful, educated, strong black woman, and she would not make a fool out of herself or embarrass her friend by cussing this man out and making a scene.

Sweet baby Jesus, give me the strength not to punch this man in his throat, Korrine thought to herself.

Before she could snap on the stranger, a deep, sultry voice came from somewhere behind her. "Hey, man, I think it's time for you to get lost. I believe the lady said she didn't want to dance with you."

The stranger started to say something when he looked up...and up some more...to where the voice was coming from. Whoever he saw, he didn't want to deal with, so he put his hands up in defeat and quickly scurried away.

Korrine knew exactly who the voice belonged to. With the stranger gone, she no longer had a buffer. She turned slowly to face the voice.

There he was standing masculine and strong; his presence was almost too overpowering. Korrine's heart started to flutter as she took him in. He was dressed in a midnight black suit that had to be tailored just for him. The slim cut of the pants hugged his muscular thighs, and the jacket hung just right. The crisp light blue button up was opened at the top with just a peek of light brown hair that covered his muscular chest. His chiseled jaw was soften by the broad smile, and his deep dimples that would make any woman melt were on full display while his dark brown eyes twinkled with mischief. His brown hair had that tousled look that fell slightly in his eyes. It was long at the top and short on the sides that gave him a slightly edgy look. Even his cologne had Korrine's head swimming. He smelled fresh with a hint of spicy sweetness. Yes, Antonio Cameron was trouble!

"Tony," Korrine greeted as she looked up into his smiling face.

"Korrine," Tony replied with a sly smile.

Tony perused Korrine's body slowly. Looking at her from toe to head, taking in her smooth chocolate brown skin covered by the red lace that left enough to the imagination but made a man hurt wanting to see more, he licked his lips in appreciation.

Korrine shifted, feeling the heat rise in her face at Tony's obvious perusal and from his overwhelming sexiness. Korrine took a deep breath, getting a hold of her hormones before she spoke again.

"Thanks for that, but I had it all under control, really," Korrine shouted over the loud music.

Tony quirked an eyebrow at her. "Well, it looked like you were fine until 'Mr. Grabass' had his hands all over you," Tony nearly growled in response.

"Ummm, o-okay, I was fine," Korrine stuttered thrown off by Tony's comment, and did he growl? Was he watching her? How did he know she was having fun before "Grabass" came along?

"So how about we continue with the fun, shall we? Want a dance?" Tony asked with mischief in his eyes.

Korrine was lost in thought. *Oh shit! If I dance with Tony, that means close personal space, bodies touching, rubbing, caressing. Shit! I can't touch him right now with all these people around. I just might jump this man right here on this damn dance floor. He looks so good...better than I remember...As much as I thought I had the curve of his jaw and the hard muscular lines of his body memorized, those memories have nothing on the big piece of juiciness standing before me. Damn! Did I mention he looks good!*

"Korrine?...Korrine?"

"Huh?" *Crap was he talking to me, and I was just standing here gaping at him?* Korrine cleared her throat. "I'm sorry. I think I need a drink if you don't mind."

A slow, wicked smile graced Tony's beautiful face. "No, sweetness, I don't mind. I would love to get you a drink." He grabbed her by the hand to lead her off the dance floor. Upon contact, Korrine felt a zap that ran down her spine and directly to her soft spot. That's why she tried so hard to stay away from this man; one simple act of hand-holding and she knew she was going to have to change her panties. She definitely needed more to drink.

Tony led Korrine to the bar where he ordered more shots of tequila. After the fourth shot, Korrine lost count. She was having a great time, and couldn't remember the last time she had so much fun. They eventually found their way to the VIP section where even Lo and Brandon joined in the shot taking. Tony had her wrapped in his arms as they cozily sat in the VIP. Korrine was so relaxed and the more she drank, the looser she felt, so she continued to drink more and more.

****

Korri was uncomfortable; her usually luxurious bed didn't feel the same. *Did I drink so much last night that my bed feels different, and why is it so dang hot? Who turned on the heat? It's May in Texas. Why is it so hot?!* Korri's mind raced and her head pounded. She slowly opened her eyes and... *Oh shit!* The hard-muscled leg and arm wrapped around her body explained why she was so hot.

Antonio freakin' Cameron! I knew I shouldn't have "let loose!" What the hell was I thinking? I've never had a one night stand. How am I supposed to sneak out when this big tank of a man has me pinned to the dang mattress?! Okay, Korrine, calm down. This is what you wanted...Let loose and have some fun...Calm down...Calm... Korrine's mind was screaming with so many questions that she failed to notice that Tony was awake and watching her with that ever-present look of mischief in his eyes.

"Good morning, sweet Korrine," Tony said while licking his lips.

Korrine shuddered. *Why does he have to say my name so sexy?* Even though he had just woke up, the deep rumble of his voice and the sexy pout of his full lips as he said her name made her heart beat faster. She cleared her throat. "Morning. I didn't realize you were awake."

She studied him a little, wondering how she ended up in bed with such a beautiful man and not remember a damn thing about it. His hard chest and chiseled abs were on full display, and those damn lips were so full and kissable looking. But she had to get the hell out of dodge before she attacked his fine ass, but how was she going to do that?

"Hmm, I see. Planning your escape, were you?" Tony laughed.

How the hell did he know that? Korrine thought to herself.

Tony laughed again. Oh shoot, maybe I didn't think that after all. Korrine hung her head in embarrassment. If her complexion was a little lighter, she would've been bright red. She was never so thankful for her mocha colored skin than at that moment.

"Uh, look, I don't know the protocol for this sort of thing, so..." Korrine let her words trail off.

"Oh, sweet, sweet Korrine, what exactly do you think we did last night?" Tony said with a cheeky smile.

"Well, since we woke up together, I figured we had sex last night," Korrine responded, more than embarrassed.

"You figured? I might be a lot of things, sweetness, but a lousy lay is *not* one of them," Tony replied slightly annoyed.

"I didn't mean to offend you. I just assumed. I never said you were lousy," Korrine said with her own annoyance starting to show.

"Sweetness, if we slept together…believe me, no matter how drunk off your sexy little ass you were, you would definitely remember."

"Oookay, so what happened? Because I really don't remember. I haven't been that drunk since I was a co-ed at college." Korrine said still feeling both embarrassed and annoyed. She felt embarrassed because she had to look a hot mess, and annoyed because she was never so drunk that she couldn't remember what happened. What thirty-one-year-old woman did that type of thing? Certainly not her.

"Korrine, I assure you nothing inappropriate happened with us last night. If you haven't noticed, you are fully clothed. We drank, laughed, and had a great time at my little cousin's birthday."

"Uuhhh," Korrine groaned. "I'm such a bad friend. I was supposed to be there for Lo, and I get drunk and end up in bed with her cousin. And what about B? What is he going to say? Shit!"

"Korrine, relax, okay? Lo was fine. She was taking shots with us, and who the hell is B?" Tony asked, feeling some kind of way about a mere mention of another man from a woman he spent most of the night wrapped around.

Korrine sighed in relief. *At least she didn't leave her friend on her birthday, and was that annoyance at the mention of Brandon? Hmmmm...interesting.*

Korrine raised a perfectly arched brow. "Well, I'm glad nothing happened and that I didn't leave Lo on her big day. I guess I should say thanks for taking care of me last night. But, if I remember correctly, a large men's t-shirt is not what I had on last night."

Tony smirked. "What kind of host would I be if my guest was uncomfortable in any way? Besides, as beautiful as you looked in that hot little number you had on last night, I didn't think you would want to ruin it by sleeping in it...and...again, who is B?"

Is he jealous? Interesting indeed. *Why would a man like Tony be jealous of anybody?*

Korrine smiled a saccharine sweet smile and replied, "Well, again, thank you for... you know... undressing me and making me 'comfortable' in your home."

Korrine deliberately didn't answer Tony's question about Brandon. She noticed how "uncomfortable" he was with the simple mention of another man. There's the arrogance showing its ugly head. She knew it wouldn't take long for him to show his true colors. How can she, a measly mortal woman, think of another when this God of a man was in her presence? He was so irritating. Even though she wouldn't, no couldn't, think of any other man while lying beside a naked chest as glorious as the one before her, she couldn't help but push his buttons just a little. She was irritating herself. Why play games with a man she didn't plan on ever sharing a bed with again? *Damn, I'm petty.*

Korrine sighed, "B is my best friend. He escorted me to the party last night, but we lost each other in the crowd. I should actually call him. He's probably been blowing up my cell."

Tony still had a frown on his face, which Korri thought was sexy. *Dang, get it together, girl. Stop lusting over this man, and get a move on.*

Before she could move, Tony spoke. "If 'B' is the guy from last night, he was with Lo. He said he had somewhere to be, kissed you good night, and left you with Lauryn. What kind of man leaves his date with someone else?"

"The kind that has known his date for seventeen years and left her in the very capable hands of 'The Lauryn Cameron.' Besides…like I said…best friend."

Tony's frowned lessened, but he still wasn't completely satisfied with her answer. But he let it go…for now.

DESIGNER DESIRES

CHAPTER 4

Tony

It had been a month since Tony woke up wrapped around one of the sexiest bodies he had ever seen...or felt, for that matter. Now Tony was no slob; he had beautiful women all the time. Models, actresses, pop stars; you name it, he had them. But Korrine; she was something special. Tony couldn't put his finger on what it was about Korrine Taylor that made him lose all thought and control over his body. Yes, she was beautiful and undeniably sexy, but she had an endearing quality; a sweetness he couldn't deny. She was strong willed and stubborn, which is why she shouldn't be worth the hassle; but, for some reason, she was. Tony was a fun loving kinda guy. He didn't need to settle down with anyone; there were far too many beautiful women in the world to savor.

As a sports agent with his own firm, Tony was very successful. He didn't need his family's fortune; he had his own. With the money he had, he could have as much fun as he wanted. "Work hard and play harder" was the motto he lived by. He had beautiful women throwing themselves at him, but he couldn't get Korrine off his mind. She looked so damn gorgeous in that red dress. It hugged her curves without being tight. But damn, when she turned around, the back of that dress had him instantly hard. He was across the room watching the sway of her hips, arms in the air, the look of pure bliss on her face. He felt like a damn stalker watching without letting her know he was there.

She just looked so free and relaxed; he had never seen her like that. She was usually so uptight and stressed. That's why, every time he saw her, he would flirt with her. She would always get so flustered. He loved to tease her, never thinking of her as anything but Lauryn's friend, until one day when he saw her at work. He went to her studio in Addison to pick up Lo, and there she was...messy bun on top of her head...pouty lips wrapped around a pencil deep in thought. All she had on was a tank top and jeans...nothing special...but she looked so beautiful. Then she looked up at him and smiled the brightest smile he had ever seen, it clicked. He had to have Korrine Taylor; she had to be his.

The first thing he had to figure out was how to get Korrine to loosen up again. He had spoken to her a few times after that night they spent together, and he even ran into her at a couple of events around town, but she seemed to always be on guard when he was around. He even tried to get her to go to dinner with him, but she always declined, saying that she was busy with her work. Tony understood that Korrine was an up and coming designer and he didn't want to be a distraction, but she was distracting him by being on his mind all the time. He had to do something to get her to let her guard down around him again. So he decided the best way to do that was to get her out at a party. He needed to get an event planned anyway for a new recruit he had just signed, and it was the perfect opportunity for him to get Korrine out, and he knew just who to call to get both done.

"Hey, my wonderful baby cousin," Tony greeted with a fake sweetness.

"Tony?" Lauryn questioned.

"Of course. Who else would it be?" Tony asked.

"What is it that you want, my wonderful older cousin?" Lauryn asked sensing a favor coming.

"Look, I need a party thrown. Better yet, I need you to throw a party."

"Now you know as well as anyone that I love to throw a party. But why, prêtell, are *you* asking *me* to throw a party?" Lauryn asked.

"I just need you to organize this shindig. I don't have the time. I actually work for a living," Tony stated in a smug tone.

"For someone that needs my help, you are pretty loose with the insults, dear cousin," Lauryn said in a smug tone of her own.

"There there, baby cousin, you know I didn't mean anything by that. But we both know your work is playing."

Lauryn laughed. "You're right, so when do you need this party?"

"Saturday," Tony stated simply.

"This Saturday?" Lauryn questioned.

"Yep."

"Like in two days, Saturday?!" Lauryn squealed.

"Yep."

"Oookay!" Lauryn huffed. "But it's going to cost you!"

"Of course it will. Oh and one more thing; I need you to make sure that you have a VIP guest list. This party is to promote my new signing of a new quarterback," Tony instructed.

Tony sat back in his chair with a satisfied grin across his modelesque face. He was confident that now that Lo was on board with throwing this party, he would have another chance at the unobtainable Ms. Taylor.

****

Saturday had come quickly and Lauryn had done a damn fine job. She should really be an event planner, but who could get her to work? If anyone mentioned job, she would go screaming from the premises. It was a smaller affair than Lo's own birthday party, but it was full of VIP's and the night was a hit. Tony promoted the hell out of his new star and even got some potential leads for new clients.

All in all, it was a good night. Korrine was there, looking stunning. She had on tight white pants and a matching white top with a tiny bit of midriff showing. She had on the sexiest heels that made her a good four inches taller. Damn, she had some beautiful legs even covered up by the pants; Tony couldn't help but imagine them wrapped around him. Shit, if he stayed on this line of thinking, he was going to have a hard-on in the middle of his own party. *What am I? A teenager? Shit...get it together, man,* Tony thought to himself.

Lauryn was in her element, partying it up like only she could, when Tony saw her with Korrine. He made his way over to them. He greeted Lauryn with a hug and a kiss on the cheek, thanking her for her help, and then he turned his attention to Korrine. Smiling devilishly, he gave her a long tight hug, lavishing in the feel of her soft curves against his hard body. She gave him a shy smile and he kissed her on the cheek, thanking her for coming. He then escorted both of them to the bar, getting them a drink before he was called away to greet some more of his guests.

While talking to some of his clients, Tony noticed that both Korrine and Lauryn seemed to be having a good time. When he was finally able to get away from schmoozing with his VIP's, he noticed that Lauryn was off being Lauryn, so he decided to seek out Korrine. But when he tried to approach her, she always seemed to get lost in the crowd. He didn't know if she was intentionally avoiding him or not. They had had more than a couple conversations via text and calls. She seemed to be fine after their platonic night together, so he didn't know why she seemed to be avoiding him now. He didn't get her, but chasing a woman is not something he did. And as much as he had the urge, he would take it slow with sweet Korrine.

Not long after, he spotted her again; the look of rage he had on his face when he saw another guy wrapped around Korrine would've scared the toughest man. Her time was being "occupied" by someone he wasn't particularly fond of. She was laughing, dancing, and grinding on one of his VIPs for what seemed like forever, and it was starting to piss Tony off. He knew she didn't know the guy because Tony himself knew exactly who he was; but to be strangers, they sure looked awfully cozy.

Jeffery Langston was a first class putz. He was what people would call a silver spooner. Jeff was from Georgia, and his family and Tony's knew each other. He was the type of guy who thought the world owed him something because his parents gave him everything. Even as a grown man, he still didn't work. He had spent years just hanging around and going from city to city partying. However, Jeff seemed to have settled in Dallas, and he looked to have his sights on Korri.

Finally, Korrine stopped dancing with Jeff and Tony was relieved. Now that Korrine was finally alone, Tony was staring at her and their eyes finally met. She smiled that breathtaking smile and his mood instantly lifted. Maybe she didn't run from him earlier; maybe it was his imagination running away with him, and she wasn't trying to avoid him. She looked relaxed like she had a couple of drinks, but she definitely wasn't drunk like the last time he saw her.

Tony was like a heat seeking missile, and the heat he was seeking was radiating from Korrine. She was standing at the bar when he approached her.

"Hey there, sweetness. It looks like you're having a good time tonight," Tony whispered in Korrine's ear.

Korrine visibly shuddered. He loved when she did that. It was such a turn on.

"Tony, nice party," Korrine smiled. "I'm having a great time, actually. Lauryn did a great job. She really should be a party planner."

Tony brushed his hand down Korrine's arm, and she gave him that wide-eyed look that he loved so much, as goose bumps popped up on her skin. He loved how she reacted to him. How did he not notice this before? Well, he sure as hell was taking notice now. He leaned down and was about to whisper in her ear again when he was interrupted.

"Hey, Antonio. Great party," Jeff, the putz that was cozying up to Korrine all night, greeted with a smirk.

This asshole knew exactly what he was doing. Nobody but Tony's father called him Antonio. He was already on thin ice for grinding on Korrine, and now he was irritating him again. This shit was not to be tolerated.

"Jeff...having a good time?" Tony stood sliding his hand possessively to the small of Korrine's back. The move didn't go unnoticed, and Jeff lifted an eyebrow.

"Yeah, I was actually having a great time with the beautiful Korrine," Jeff replied looking from Korrine to Tony and back again.

Korrine shifted, looking a little uncomfortable. She cleared her throat and said, "Excuse me, gentlemen. I need to go powder my nose."

Tony leaned down and whispered in her ear, "Of course, sweetness. But please hurry back because I owe you a drink." Korrine smiled nervously and quickly walked toward the restrooms.

Jeff gave Tony a look of outrage. Tony passively looked back at Jeff. They stared at one another for what seemed like hours, but couldn't have been more than seconds. They let the tension build until Jeff finally broke the silence under Tony's intense gaze.

"What was that?" Jeff scoffed. "You know damn well I was going to bag that hot piece. That ass is as good as mine, and you know it. She couldn't wait to take me home, so are you cock-blocking because you don't have enough toys to play with? Not getting enough attention from the rest of these bitches? I've been working her all night, and the "Great Antonio" will not fuck this up for me."

Tony tried to keep his cool. He clenched and unclenched his fists trying to rein in his temper. He had a lot of clients as guests and he didn't want to get into something physical with this asshole. He knew that Lauryn only invited Jeff because their families had known each other for years, but this pretentious jerk was digging a deep hole. His comments about Korrine were pushing Tony's hospitality. He had already been grinding on Korrine all night, and now he wanted to make offhanded comments?

Time to put this motherfucker in his place.

"Jeff…no real man would ever call Korrine Taylor anything but gorgeous," Tony growled with unmistakable fury. "She's nobody's toy, bitch, or anything else your fucked up little mind can think of. What I suggest to you, because you have pushed the limits of my patience, is to get the fuck out of my face and party before I lose my cool."

For a brief second, Jeff had a look of fear in his eyes before he quickly recovered and his expression went cold. But he didn't catch himself quite quickly enough because Tony saw the fear, and he was glad because he meant what he said. Korrine would not be disrespected in his presence, and at that moment he wanted to really whoop his ass!

Jeff smirked at Tony and said, "I was leaving this poor ass excuse for an event anyways. Although the caliber of tail is okay, I need something a little more blonde to sate my appetite, but I will be seeing you."

"No, I'll be seeing you, Jeffery," Tony replied coldly.

Jeff shrugged and darted away just before Korrine came walking back from the restroom.

"Oh, is Jeff leaving?" Korrine asked curiously.

"Yep, he had to run," Tony responded dryly.

"Hmmm, did *you* have anything to do with that, Mr. Cameron?" Korrine asked smiling, knowing all too well that Tony was the reason Jeff looked like the hounds of hell were nipping at his heels. He was nearly running from the bar, not even stopping to say goodbye.

"Who me? Naaah…" Tony replied changing the subject. "I owe you a drink, sweetness. Lo would kill me if I didn't give you what I promised."

"And what exactly did you promise her?" Korrine asked.

"A good time and as many drinks as you wanted, my sweetness," Tony answered giving Korrine his big dimpled smile.

Korrine grinned and let him get her a drink. Before long, they were laughing and talking. Korrine actually relaxed and realized she didn't have to be drunk.

"You owe me a dance, sweetness," Tony said pulling Korrine by the hand.

This time when Tony asked her to dance, she went willingly...not over thinking anything, but just going with the flow.

Korrine let him pull her to the floor. He surprised her with his rhythm. *Yea, I got moves, sweetness,* Tony thought to himself looking into Korrine's eyes. She raised an eyebrow at him, and he smiled. He pulled her closer, grinding his growing muscle into her. She whimpered at the contact, and he smirked. *Ms. Korrine and her noises are going to do me in. I will have her tonight,* Tony thought with a wicked grin on his face.

Korrine let him grind on her. She knew she was acting out of character, but she didn't care. She was actually having fun. After the night they spent together, she knew he was a gentleman. He could've easily taken advantage of her without a second thought, but he didn't, and she liked that. Under all that arrogance, there might have been a nice guy after all. Plus he wasn't hard on the eyes, and she needed to get her groove back. So why the hell not?

Korrine slowly caressed Tony's chest as they swayed to the music. She could feel the heat coming off his body, making her own temperature rise.

"So, Tony, I must admit that when I first met you, I didn't think you were a very nice guy."

"Me? Why would you say that? I'm nice to all the girls, sweetness," Tony replied with a smirk.

Korrine chuckled, "Yeah, and that's one of the reasons I didn't consider you as being nice. Because of all of 'your girls'."

Tony smiled in response, "Korrine, I am a man. I appreciate beautiful women. You can't blame a guy for that. Yes, I like to have a good time, but believe me when I say that 'my girls' know exactly what they are getting with me. I don't play games and I'm not out to hurt anyone. Any woman that gets involved with me knows that from the start. I want you. I have for a very long time."

Korrine knew then that she didn't just like Tony for his beautiful face and muscular body. She saw that the man within was someone honest that knew exactly what he wanted. Yes, he was arrogant, but unlike her ex, he was up front and didn't want to play games, so she wouldn't play games either. It was time for her to take a risk for once.

"Let's get out of here," Korrine told Tony as she wrapped her arms around his waist.

"Uh...Sure let's..." It was Tony's turn to stutter, being momentarily caught off guard by her suggestion.

Tony led her off the dance floor, saying goodbye to business contacts as he rushed her to the door. He was trying not to be seen by Lo, who would want to know where they were going and why they were leaving so soon. More to the point, she would want all of Korrine's attention. Now that he had it, he wasn't giving it up. Korrine wasn't just another conquest. No, she was special. He would make sure not to screw up this time because she was willingly going with him. She even suggested it. He couldn't get out of there fast enough.

CHAPTER 5

Tony

"Welcome back to my humble abode," Tony said while opening the door to his house.

Korrine grinned. "Thanks."

He could tell she was a little nervous. She didn't have that much to drink, so the liquid courage she had the last time wasn't there. However, she still looked relaxed, and that's what he truly wanted.

Tony moved behind Korrine, wrapping his arms around her waist and bending to kiss her neck. She moaned and arched her back, giving him greater access. He began to lick and suck at her skin; the taste of her was making him lose control. He growled a low deep sound that had Korrine squirming in his arms. He pulled her tighter against him, grinding his erection into her ass. She turned to face him, grabbing his upper arms and squeezing his muscular biceps. She slid her hands upward, caressing his neck as she leaned in and licked him.

He growled again and pressed his lips to her mouth in one quick swoop. His kiss was hungry and urgent, like a starving man receiving his last meal. Their tongues battled for supremacy; probing, sucking, and tasting one another. Neither could get enough. Control was out the window...it was lost.

Korrine ripped her mouth away from his, gasping for breath with desired filled eyes. Tony's brown eyes were practically black, with lust seeping from his every pore. They stared at each other for a moment before Korrine unconsciously licked her lips, causing Tony to moan and pull her tighter before pushing her shirt above her breasts.

Korrine was completely exposed...not having on a bra. Her chest heaved up and down with each breath. Tony leaned down, grabbing both her breasts in his huge hands and licking from one to the other.

Korrine sighed lustfully. Tony smiled around a mouth full of nipple. He moved from one to the other, lavishing attention on both equally, tweaking one hard nub...all the while licking the other until switching. Back and forth he went until Korrine's body was humming with anticipation.

Tony grabbed her wrists, pinning them above her head as he backed her against the wall. His other hand began traveling down her body until he reached the button of her white pants. He unbuttoned and unzipped them slowly as if he was unwrapping a gift.

She was so small that he could reach the length of her body with just a simple bend. He let go of her hands and reached down so he could drag her pants down over her hips and over her luscious deep brown thighs. Korrine helped, kicking off her shoes and sliding her pants the rest of the way off. She was standing before Tony with her breasts out, wearing only a thin lacy thong. He smiled that wicked smile and slid his hand down her toned belly, rubbing the trim of her lacy panties. *These aren't going to last,* Tony thought.

He could smell her arousal, which was increasing his own. She was hypnotic. He grabbed the panties and ripped them from her body, exposing her flesh. He lowered his hand to her now dripping wet center. Tony ran his finger along her slit, teasing her with light touches until Korrine was grinding against his finger trying to get him to stop teasing her.

He chuckled. "So eager, my sweetness," Tony came from his throat in a low sexy tone.

"Please…." Korrine pleaded.

"Please what, sweetness? What do you want me to do? Do you want me to stop?" Tony asked.

"No! Please give me what I want, Tony," Korrine pleaded.

"What do you want, baby?" Tony coaxed. "Tell me what you want."

"I want you! I need you, Tony!" Korrine moaned in a voice that was raspy with yearning.

Tony plunged his finger into her hungry opening. Pushing it deep within her, he worked his finger in and out, adding another while rubbing her sensitive nub with his thumb. Korrine began to grind harder, her breath hitching, so Tony began to speed up.

"Tony...It feels so good...I'm going to...OOOOHHH SSSHIIIIT!" Korrine hissed out.

"Cum for me baby!" Tony urged her, continuing to move his fingers with precision.

Korrine's orgasm hit her hard; she couldn't control her breathing and her head was spinning.

Tony grabbed her. "I'm just getting started with you, sweetness." As he hoisted her up, her legs instinctively wrapped around his waist with his slack clad erection probing at her core. He was hard as a rock and couldn't wait to get into her waiting body. He walked them to his bedroom, kissing passionately the entire way. He lowered her to the bed, taking off her top. She was completely naked, waiting and willing for him to devour. She smiled a shy smile that was both innocent and sexy. He looked at her, slipping his finger in his mouth and moaning.

"You taste exactly how I knew you would...sweet," Tony told her with assurance.

"Tony?" Korrine sighed.

"Yes, baby?" Tony questioned.

"I'm naked, and you have all of your clothes on. I need you to stop with all the talking and fuck me... *now!*" Korrine said with a growl of her own.

Maybe that wasn't a look of innocence because that was the hottest fuckin' thing ever, Tony thought, undressing in record time.

He slipped on a condom and hovered over Korrine. She opened her legs wider to accommodate his large frame. She looked down and gasped, instantly tensing. Tony was not an averaged sized man in height, weight, or girth. He was huge.

"Ah, are you shocked. I see you didn't know a white boy would be packing," Tony teased with a smirk trying to get Korrine to relax. It worked. Korrine let out a chuckle and then a moan, as Tony eased in her slowly. He moaned his pleasure when he was in all the way to the hilt. He started moving at a slow grinding pace, their bodies moving in rhythm with one another. Tony lifted her legs higher, placing them in the crook of his arm to put her in a better position to receive his massive member. Korrine rocked up to meet his thrusts. Tony started moving faster inside her, rolling his hips and pushing deeper and deeper. He brought her to the brink of another orgasm before slowing down, pulling almost completely out of her. Korrine whined her disapproval. Tony chuckled, leaning down to pull her pouting bottom lip in his mouth. He nibbled and sucked on her lip, all while swiveling and rolling his hips in a mind-numbing rhythm that brought Korrine right to where he wanted her to be…on the verge of madness…just like him.

"Turn over, sweetness. I need to see that beautiful ass in the air."

Korrine immediately turned over, lying flat on her stomach and looking back at Tony over her shoulder. Tony stood for a moment, looking at her beautiful body and rubbing his shaft up and down in a slow rhythm. He was becoming impossibly harder just looking at her. Tony pulled Korrine by her waist, leaning her up so that she was on all fours. He reached down and slid himself in her wet core, easily moving within her. He reached around her, rubbing her clit while keeping up the mind blowing pace from behind. Her ass was hitting his pelvis, jiggling with every hard penetrating thrust. It was driving Tony crazy that her perfect round ass with smooth chocolate colored skin was moving in time with him. He was completely lost in the moment. Korrine's loud moans regained his focus, and Tony smacked her ass to make her scream. He removed his hand from her clit and up to her breasts, which were bouncing wildly with each pump of his hips. He squeezed and tweaked her nipples, causing her to throw her head back and pant for more. Tony guided her to lie down on her stomach while still inside her. He couldn't bear to lose contact with her at this moment. He placed his knees on the outside of her body while arching her back and pulling her ass up to meet him. He moved her body up and down, grinding his shaft into her over and over. Pushing and pulling, moaning and groaning...the sensation was like none he had ever felt before. Her body felt so good to him; she was so hot and tight. She was squeezing the life out of his organ. He could hardly stand the pleasure of it, but he didn't want to come yet. So he abruptly pulled out, turning her over in one swift move.

Korrine was speechless. He was tossing her around like a ragdoll, and she couldn't get enough. In the next moment Tony was attacking her lips, moving his tongue in and out of her mouth while firmly massaging her breasts. He slowly moved down her body, kissing and licking her skin until he got to the apex of her thighs. He could smell the mix of their lovemaking, and it turned him on even more. He dipped his head, getting a quick taste of her essence. It was driving him insane; he had to be back inside her. So he quickly pushed in her, rolling over so that Korrine could be on top. He sat up with Korrine in his lap and, even though she was on top, Tony was still in control. He pushed into her while she bounced up and down on his massive shaft, her arms wrapped around his neck and broad shoulders. He pulled her head down to kiss her lips. The desire that they both felt was undeniable. It was as if neither wanted to let go and go over the edge. Both of them were holding on to that carnal desire to stay in the moment.

Tony kept up the pace, speeding up and then slowing down over and over again until he finally couldn't hold on any longer. He sped up, thrusting harder into Korrine's willing pussy. He continued kissing, licking, and tasting until he could feel his balls tighten and his shaft becoming even harder.

"Oh shit, sweetness," Tony moaned as he continued to pump into her. "I'm about to…uhhh…Koooorrrrine…shit…"

Korrine let out a loud scream releasing her second climax of the night. Tony stayed inside her, slowly pumping in and out while trying to come down off his powerful orgasm. He could still feel her inner muscles clenching and unclenching while the spasms were holding him hostage.

Their breathing started to slowly return to normal. Tony reluctantly pulled out of Korrine, both feeling the loss immediately. Tony got up and removed the condom, tossing it into the trash. He returned to bed, pulling Korrine into his chest and kissing the top of her head before pulling the comforter over their exhausted bodies.

CHAPTER 6

Tony

Tony went into this with the idea of having Korrine once to get her out of his system. But there was no way he could have her just once…there was just no way. Tony was normally a love 'em and leave 'em type of guy. He wasn't the relationship type; it just wasn't who he was. Plus, he had a tall wall up around his heart.

He saw his cousin and best friend, Jake, get his heart demolished; he was a broken man for so long. He knew he would never want to go through that kind of pain. After three years, Jake still didn't date. He was no longer the fun-loving guy Tony grew up with.

He couldn't help his cousin, and it seemed like forever before Jake got any control back over his life after one woman destroyed it. Tony could never let that happen. He loved to be in control. The idea of not having it and, worse yet, giving the control to someone else was more than he could handle. The control for Tony started when he was very young. His parents, although he loved them dearly - well, he loved his mother anyway- tried to control every aspect of his life. He learned young that if he didn't stand up for himself, he would always be living for others. He was driven to succeed, not wanting to rely on his father's money because that would mean following his rules and he couldn't bring himself to do that. However, Korrine was making him lose his precious control, and he had to get it back. Every time he was around her, his senses would go haywire. She made him want to take her wherever they were, crowd be damned.

They were having so much fun together. It had been over two months of them "hanging out." For some reason, that's what Korrine always called their time together: "hanging out." She never said they were dating, which essentially was what they were doing. At least that's what Tony felt. Any free moment he had, he would call or text her. But it wasn't just him; she would call and text him just as much.

They would have dinner, go to the movies, or just stay in and watch TV. They would even cuddle sometimes, which was something Tony definitely didn't do. He rarely even brought a woman back to his place. It was easier to go to theirs, make up an excuse, or slip out and just leave them. But he didn't want to slip out or make excuses when it came to Korrine. All he wanted to do was be with her and *in* her...all the time!

One night they were out having dinner, the conversation was flowing, and they couldn't keep their hands off each other. But then they were approached by an acquaintance of Korrine's. At least that's what she called him: "an *acquaintance.*" But he acted more familiar than Tony was comfortable with. Steve was his name. He stood around 5'11" with sandy blond hair that was cut low. He had a long nose, but it fit his slim face with a dimple in his chin. His hazel eyes were round and doe-like that gave him a boyish look. He had a slender muscular build as if he ran, but didn't lift weights. Steve had a confidence that women loved.

He walked up and smiled a wicked smile at Korrine; a smile that Tony was all too familiar with. It was the same smile he gave her when he thought about how sexy she was without her even knowing it.

He really didn't like this guy.

Steve cleared his throat and, when Korrine saw him, her face lit up. It *actually* lit up. *Who is this asshole?* Tony thought.

She practically jumped into his arms to hug him. Over her shoulder, Steve smirked at Tony and he instantly went on alert. When she regained her composure and sat back in her chair, Tony immediately placed an arm around her back and extended his hand to Steve to introduce himself when Korrine introduced Tony as a friend.

Tony lifted an eyebrow at her, and Steve smirked again.

I hate it when people smirk at me. Why didn't she introduce me as her boyfriend or, at the very least, her date? And why in the hell does it bother me so much that she didn't? The thoughts that crossed Tony's mind made him slightly uncomfortable. He didn't want to be her boyfriend...or did he?

Before he would stake his claim, he had to let Korrine know who was in charge of her body because she seemed to have forgotten. Tony leaned in, kissed her just behind her ear and whispered, "Friend, huh?" She instantly shuddered, and he gave her his biggest dimpled smile before excusing himself from the table to take an important call.

Steve didn't miss Korrine's reaction, and it was Tony's turn to smirk. Tony just stepped away to take his call, giving Korrine and her "acquaintance" sometime before he busted this dipshit's bubble.

"Steve, how have you been? It's been what...almost three years...since I've seen you?" Korrine asked.

"Yep, nearly three years," Steve replied. "I've been doing well Korri. How have you been?" "I've been doing great, actually. My designs are doing well, and I have my own space. Everything is going great!" Korrine responded excitedly.

"I thought you would be married to what's his name by now. But I don't see a ring on that beautiful hand, so I guess that didn't happen," Steve stated with an almost glee like tone. "But I couldn't help but notice this new guy. Is he your boyfriend or something?" Steve inquired with a sneer.

"Nope, no ring; I broke up with what's his name. And, like I said, Tony is a friend," Korrine said simply.

"Hmm...I guess. So if he's just a friend, then you're finally single?" Steve asked moving closer to Korrine.

"Not exactly, but you know how it can be when you first start seeing someone," Korrine stated, shifting farther away from Steve.

"Hey, I get it. But like you said, if you just started seeing him and he's just a friend, then maybe we can go get coffee and catch up. It's been such a long time since I've lived here that I feel almost new in town. Everything is different in the DFdub," Steve chuckled trying to lighten the conversation.

Korrine hesitated. But when she saw the boyish smile Steve had on his face, she felt guilty for pushing away an old acquaintance. They could be friends this time around. Darren had been so jealous of any man that she couldn't befriend hardly anyone. "Sure, why not? Like you said, there have been a lot of changes in the DFdub," Korrine responded with a chuckle of her own.

Tony heard the exchange and felt Steve was being a bit forward for just being an acquaintance. Upon his return to the table, Korrine was sitting at a comfortable distance away from Steve. Steve didn't seem to like this fact, so Tony sat close to Korrine, leaning in to kiss her neck. He knew his little display worked because he knew *his* sweetness. Make no mistake she was *his*, even if she didn't want to admit it yet.

Korrine was just about to say something to Steve when Tony gave her a panty dropping, heat-filled look and Korrine lost whatever she was about to say…again a fact that Steve didn't seem to appreciate.

Korrine stuttered, "Uh… Um… Steve, Tony and I were waiting on the check so we could leave."

Steve frowned. "Not a problem. I will definitely be keeping in touch since I am permanently back in town."

Steve then leaned down to hug Korrine before extending his hand to Tony. "It was nice meeting you, man," he uttered with a smile that didn't reach his eyes.

Tony simply nodded, not giving a reply.

Korrine cleared her throat and narrowed her eyes at Tony before the two men finally let go of the firm handshake, with Steve departing with another hug for Korrine.

Nope, don't like this asshole at all, Tony thought before placing a possessive hand around Korrine's waist and pulling her to him. She raised an eyebrow at Tony's possessive move, and he just smiled down at her while stealing a kiss from her plump lips. The look of wanting returned to her face, and he knew he had successfully distracted her.

That night after they left the restaurant and returned to his place, Tony wanted to have a conversation about this Steve guy.

"So, how do you know this Steve?" Tony asked with a quirked eyebrow.

Korrine replied, "I met him at the coffee shop around the corner from my apartment. He owned a real estate company, but he moved to Houston a couple years before and we lost touch. Why do you ask?"

Tony shrugged his shoulders. "He just seemed awfully familiar. Did you two date?"

It was Korrine's turn to quirk an eyebrow. "No, we were casual friends, hanging out here and there, but that was all. We never dated."

Tony didn't look convinced.

"Look, Tony, I was just excited to see him because it had been such a long time," Korrine convinced him. "He's a nice guy, just an old friend."

Tony nodded. He could understand what she was saying, but the only problem was that Tony didn't think that Steve thought of Korrine as an acquaintance. Tony knew that Steve wanted in her panties, and Tony wasn't the sharing type. Korrine and her panties were his, and this douchebag needed to be made aware of that ASAP.

CHAPTER 7

Korrine

After the night they ran into Steve, Tony was acting a little unusual. He seemed upset that she hadn't put a label on what they were. Korrine had just said they were friends because she didn't want to hurt his feelings or, better yet, his ego by calling it a fling. The sex was incredible, and she couldn't get enough of Tony. Any time they were in the same room, she just wanted to rip his clothes off and then her own. Her sense of awareness of him was unbelievable; whenever he was near, she could feel his presence. It was something that she never felt before, not even with Darren, and that's what scared her the most. She couldn't get distracted with another man. She couldn't lose herself, not again.

The time they spent together was so much fun. She had never been so relaxed. And to be totally honest, she was more creative. Her juices were definitely flowing, in more ways than one. This is what she needed—no strings attached fun, incredible sex, and to relax—so that she could create more killer designs. So why was Tony all of a sudden trying to make it more?

She couldn't spend time worrying about what Tony was thinking. Besides, he was out of town on business, and, while he was away, she really needed to focus on her work. Korrine had just gotten a new upscale client. The pop star was an up and coming diva. She was just nominated for a prestigious award and had the number three hit on the music charts. To have one of her designs on a red carpet that big would be spectacular, so she didn't have time to entertain what Tony was thinking about; she had work to do.

Korrine was having another late night at her studio, and she was exhausted. The dress she was designing for the pop star, Tia, was nearly complete. She was proud of her progress, but she only had a couple of weeks to finish it and fit her. Hopefully, Tia would love it as much as Korrine did.

After hours of designing, Korrine was packing up for the night. She couldn't keep her eyes open, and she knew that staying any longer wouldn't do any good. She was searching for her keys when she heard a knock on her studio door. The building was secure, so she wasn't all that worried. But she wondered who it could be at this late hour when she knew Tony was out of town and Brandon was with his new boyfriend. *So who in the hell?*

When she opened the door, she was in shock. Steve stood there with his hands in his pockets, looking a little boyish. He looked up and smiled a shy smile when she opened the door.

"Hey, Steve. What are you doing here?" Korrine questioned.

"Hi, Korrine. I just opened an office in the building next door. I meant to come earlier, but I got caught up in paperwork and I no longer have your number. When I saw the light still on, I thought I'd come say hello," Steve replied, in a hurry with a frown.

"Oh, I'm sorry. I didn't mean to offend you. I was just a little taken off guard. I haven't seen you since the night at the restaurant. When was that? Three weeks ago?" Korrine stated.

"Uh, yeah. But like I said, we didn't exchange numbers, so..." Steve let his words trail off, letting the smile return to his face.

Korrine smiled. "You're right. I'm sorry, Steve. I'm exhausted with work. Again, I was just a little caught off guard with you being here. But I'm really glad you stopped by. I was just on my way out."

As Korrine started packing up, she asked Steve, "How did you know I was in this building?"

73

"Oh, I had a tour, and the leasing agent told me about the tenants. He mentioned an up and coming designer. I knew it just couldn't be you, but voila it was," Steve stated nervously.

Korrine thought Steve's over explaining seemed a bit odd, but she was too tired to question him. Steve always seemed a bit odd anyway.

"Oh, wow, it's a small world, but, like I said, I was headed out..." Korrine trailed off hinting for Steve to leave.

Steve smiled in return. "It's fine, Korri. I understand. Really, I do. How about I walk you to your car. Maybe during the week, if you have time, we can get that coffee we talked about...or maybe dinner or something."

Korrine smiled again. "I'd like that, Steve, and congrats on the new digs! This is a really nice area. You will love it here. It's such a coincidence that we are so close."

Steve smiled, but it didn't reach his eyes. He walked Korrine to her car, and they said their goodbyes.

Steve smiled a wicked smile to himself as she drove off. Korri had no idea how much he went through to get that office. After all these years, she was finally single, and she would be his. The opportunity for them to be together was finally here, and he would make sure not to let her slip through his grasp...this time. The opportunity had finally presented itself, and he had the inside track to Korrine because of his little helper. Now all she had to do was fall in line.

Korrine finally pulled into her uptown apartment, realizing that she was dog tired. Her cell phone rang. She knew exactly who it was, and her face lit up with excitement. She tried to calm herself so she wouldn't seem so eager.

Who was she kidding? Hell, she *was* eager. He had only been gone four days, and she missed him like crazy. She was trying to fool herself saying this was a fling. She knew it was more, but damn if she was ready to admit it.

"Hey, sweetness," came Tony's deep, sultry voice through the phone.

"Hey, Tony. Do you miss me?" Korrine asked in a sultry voice of her own.

"Of course I do, baby. Why else would I call so late at night?" Tony smiled.

"True," Korrine stated simply.

Tony chuckled. "So are you home yet? I didn't want to interrupt your work, but I wanted to make sure you were home safe and sound."

"Yep, I'm home finally. But you know my studio is safe. And now Steve is right next door, so he walked me to my car," Korrine replied.

Tony frowned. "Steve is in the building next door?"

"Yeah. Isn't that funny? We didn't even exchange numbers, but he happened to get the office right next door. So see; I'm surrounded by protection. No need to worry your pretty little head about me, superman," Korrine said.

Tony's frowned deepened. He didn't like this guy Steve. He didn't like him when he met him, and he didn't like that he was trying to get close to Korrine. This asshole was up to something. He needed to stay alert and do a check on this Steve character as soon as he was back from Georgia.

"Yeah, that *is* funny," Tony replied dryly.

Korrine sighed. "What is it, Tony?"

"Nothing, sweetness. It's just peculiar how he just so happens to get an office in a building so close to yours, when there are so many office spaces in the DFW," Tony stated.

"It's a coincidence, baby." Korrine sighed again.

She called him baby on purpose. It would always distract him because she didn't do it that often, usually only during sex. When she would talk dirty to him and moan "baby," he would be putty in her hands. So far it had worked every time. Hopefully, it would work this time.

"Ok, sweetness, it's a coincidence." Tony responded.

Korrine smiled to herself. The distraction worked. She was glad because the only other distraction tactic she had over the phone was her sexy come get it talk, and she was way too tired for that at this moment. But even just thinking about Tony coming and getting it was making her start to throb. She could hear his smile over the phone. *I bet those dimples are on full display.* Korrine groaned inwardly. If she thought about his dimples, it would lead to other impure thoughts, and she really needed to sleep. With Tony being gone, she couldn't get her fix until tomorrow night at the earliest.

"Well, superman, I need to go. I'm tired, and I need to take a nice hot bath before I get in the bed," Korrine said through a yawn.

Tony groaned. "Come on, sweetness. If you are trying to get me off the phone, giving me an image of your naked dripping wet body in a tub is not the way to go about it."

Korrine chuckled. "Sorry, Tony. I didn't mean to get you all hot and bothered."

"Well, sweetness, that's exactly what you did. Now I'm hard. What do you think I can do with this thing since you aren't here to…relieve me?" Tony sighed almost in agony.

Korrine moaned. "I guess you need to touch him and caress him slowly like I would if I was there with you now."

Tony was getting excited, "What else would you do? Tell me, sweetness."

Okay, come and get it talk it is...I don't know why I thought I could have a phone conversation with Tony at this time of night without it turning sexual.

Korrine started in her sexiest voice. "You know what I would do? I would grab you, stroking up and down, caressing you slowly, and letting you grow harder and harder until you're completely ready for me...you ready for me, superman? Are you hard enough to penetrate this sweetness? Huh? Can you imagine how wet I am, willing, and hot just for you?"

"Damn, baby. I'm ready. What else would you do?" Tony breathed, stroking his manhood while Korrine talked.

"I would get on top of you, slide you in, and ride you slow. Can you imagine me, baby? Riding you up and down slowly feels so good, with you sliding in and out of my wet hot pussy. Can you feel my walls pulsing with every thrust? Can you feel me getting tighter around you, speeding up? You feel so good, baby," she moaned. "Hmm...I can feel you so deep, stroking in and out of me. You fill me up, and I'm so wet for you, baby." Korrine was getting hot.

"Yes, baby, and what else will happen? Tell me, sweetness," Tony's voice was hoarse as he chased his orgasm; he was stroking up and down faster and faster.

"I feel you about to cum, baby. I feel how hard you are pulsing inside of me. I'm strangling your dick. Can you feel how tight I am? I'm ready, baby," Korrine moaned into the phone. "Are you ready?"

"I'm ready, sweetness," Tony said breathing hard.

"I'm so hot, baby...I'm going to cum!" Korrine's voice was strained as she was touching herself and rubbing her clit at a feverish pace. She could feel the mounting pleasure, and she was about to explode.

Tony moaned his release, "Shit, baby!!! Korrine that was totally fuckin' hot! I'm coming home tomorrow, and you are going to show me exactly what you just described." "It's a date," Korrine said with a tired smile before she disconnected the call. "Goodnight, superman,"

Damn, I wasn't planning on phone sex tonight. But if that means even hotter sex tomorrow, it was totally worth it.

CHAPTER 8

Korrine

The next morning, Korrine was putting finishing touches on Tia's dress in her studio when her door chimed and Steve walked in. He had a bright smile on his face and a cup of coffee in his hand.

"Hey, Korri. I thought since you looked so tired last night, I would bring you a cup of your favorite. You like caramel macchiato, right?" Steve asked with a smile.

Korrine smiled in relief. "You remembered! You are a life saver! I didn't have time to stop today."

Steve smiled again. "Anything for you, honey."

Steve had never called her honey. But Korrine tried not to over think the endearment. He was just being a nice guy, like always, she figured. Steve had always showed Korrine attention, but now it just seemed different. Yet, Korrine brushed it off. Steve was a nice guy, and that's all there was to it.

Korrine nodded her thanks, groaning as the coffee went down her throat.

"Mmmm…so good!" Korrine smiled.

Steve touched Korrine's hand. "No problem. I'm glad I can make you moan."

Korrine arched an eyebrow at Steve and the double entendre. He chuckled lightly and moved his hand away from Korrine's.

"Loosen up, Korri. I was only joking. You know me…always the joker," Steve said moving toward the door.

Korrine smiled. "You're right. Thanks again for the coffee."

"See ya around, Korri." Before Steve finished his exit he turned and said, "I have a heavy day today, but maybe we can have dinner tonight."

"Sorry, Steve. I have plans. Maybe we can do lunch in a couple of days," Korrine replied.

"Sure, in a couple of days. No problem," he told her with a forced smile.

Korrine thought the exchange was weird, but she was tired and assumed that Steve was only being helpful. She really did need to loosen up. She was doing a pretty good job since she had been seeing Tony. But she had been so driven to succeed for so long, letting loose just wasn't high on her priority list. However, that was slowly changing because of her "superman."

Korrine gave him the nickname one night after a dinner. She told him he was looking at her like he had x-ray vision. When they got to his place that night, he manhandled her like he indeed had super powers. He lifted her and tossed her around like she weighed nothing, and he made her orgasm so hard she thought she was flying....Yes; superman was a fitting nickname for Antonio Cameron.

Korrine couldn't wait for the day to be over. She finished with Tia's dress early, so she was able to fit her and get the dress to her a week ahead of schedule. Tia's award show was still two weeks away, so she wasn't sure how the dress would be received. Yet, just by word of mouth, Tia got Korrine another big client to come in for a fitting for another awards show. Korrine was on cloud nine and she couldn't have been happier, but she couldn't shake this nagging feeling that something was wrong. Something just felt off lately, and she couldn't put her finger on what. It had been a couple of weeks since Steve moved into the building next door, and he would stop by either in the morning for coffee or in the afternoon for lunch. He was normally around when Korrine was ready to leave as well, no matter what time that was. That was odd, but Korrine was thankful because she liked having someone walk her to her car. She didn't need Steve that often because Tony had been more present lately. He would come by her studio, and they would have a late dinner or they would go to her place and just hang out.

One night Korrine was leaving her studio, and Tony had a late meeting. She hadn't seen Steve all day, so she walked to her car alone. When she got to it, there was a note with a rose stuck on the windshield. *Who could this be from?* she thought as she opened the note. It read in bold letters:

YOU ARE A BEAUTIFUL WOMAN! ANY MAN WOULD BE LUCKY TO HAVE YOU. BUT YOU SHOULD HAVE HIGHER STANDARDS. I WILL SHOW YOU SOON WHAT A REAL MAN CAN DO!

Korrine was freaked out. She ran back in her studio immediately, and she then called Brandon. Because Tony was in a meeting, and she didn't want to disturb him, Brandon was her go to. When Korrine called Brandon and told him about the note, he rushed to her studio with his new boyfriend Brent in tow. The two men were worried, and they told Korrine she should call the police and report the incident. Korrine disagreed, saying she was caught off guard, but it didn't seem to be any real threat. *It was just a note…right?* But she finally reluctantly agreed to call the police after being nagged to death by her best friend; after all, she *was* still a little freaked out.

Once the police were there, they took her statement and the note as evidence.

"Ma'am, there isn't much we can do at this point," the officer stated. "At the very least, we can try to get prints."

Korrine, sighed, frustrated. "Well, what should I do if this happens again?"

"You will need to keep documentation of any type of harassment," he answered. "If you get calls, make sure you record them if you can. At the very least, write down the time and date and what was said. If there are any more notes left, be sure not to touch it, and call us immediately."

"So you're saying there's absolutely nothing you can do for me?" Korrine asked.

"With so little to go on, no, ma'am, there isn't much that can be done. This isn't considered a real threat. The note wasn't addressed to anyone specifically," the officer responded.

Later that night when Tony called to check on her, he was livid when she told him what happened. Korrine didn't understand why he was so angry with her. It was just a note and, even though it unnerved her a little, she still thought that the men in her life were overreacting. It could've been just some kids playing a bad joke or something. She hadn't seen anyone suspicious hanging around, and nothing else happened. She did get that she should have called Tony, but she didn't want to interrupt his meeting. Tony told her there was no meeting more important than her safety, and he would be at her house ASAP.

When Tony arrived at Korrine's apartment, his jacket and his tie were off and the top two buttons of his crisp white shirt were undone. He looked like he had been running his hands through his hair because it was all disheveled. But somehow the vision of him standing at her door with his hands balled into fists and his lips in almost a pout made Korrine think how deliciously sexy he looked.

Before she could take in Tony and all his glory, he stormed in, wrapped her in his arms, kicked the door shut, and pinned her against the wall, kissing her with a fierceness he had never shown her before. When he finally stopped kissing her lips, he started slowly kissing her cheeks and up to her forehead. She looked into his eyes, and there she saw a fire that was mixed with passion and what she thought could be anger. *Was he angry at her?*

"Are you all right, baby?" Tony asked Korrine while slowly releasing her from his strong arms.

"I'm fine, Tony. I promise," Korrine answered with a weak smile.

"Then why in the fuck didn't you call me, Korrine?" Tony replied in a calm voice that didn't match his words or the anger he was feeling.

"Antonio Cameron, don't you ever curse at me!" Korrine shouted.

Tony frowned, releasing her fully and starting to pace. "Korrine Taylor, I am *not* cursing at you, okay? I just want to know why you didn't call me immediately after you found the note. This is serious. I…care…a lot about you, and for someone to threaten you and you not to tell me is unacceptable!"

Korrine reached out and grabbed Tony's hand to keep him from pacing. She turned him toward her and cupped his face in her small hands. "Tony, I'm sorry. I'm really sorry. I just didn't think it was urgent enough to interrupt your meeting. Besides B came by, and I wasn't alone. The security guard was on duty, and Brandon and Brent talked me into calling the police. There isn't anything anyone can do. There wasn't a 'real threat' as the cop put it, and nobody saw anything. So I just have to be more alert. That's all."

"I get that, Korrine. But there is nothing more important than your safety. If you don't call me, how am I supposed to protect you from this psycho?" Tony asked frustrated.

"Tony, it was just a note," Korrine stated, growing exasperated.

"I don't see it as just a note, Korrine. I don't want you walking from your building at night by yourself anymore, no matter what!" Tony said with finality.

Korrine knew this "discussion" could go on all night, so she just agreed not to walk alone anymore when it got too late. She understood everyone's concern, and she wouldn't put herself in unnecessary, harmful situations. She just couldn't figure out who this person was and what they wanted from her. She had never been in a situation like this before. *Why would someone do this?*

CHAPTER 9

Korrine

It had been a couple of days since the "note incident," and Korrine was starting to feel a bit on edge. Tony was there for her though, making sure he was there when she was ready to leave her studio or making sure Brandon or the security guard was there when he couldn't be. Nothing unusual had happened—no more notes, and no suspicious people hanging around. Steve had been a bit standoffish though. When Korrine told him about the note, he didn't really have the reaction she expected. He hardly seemed concerned. But he did later apologize, saying he had a lot on his plate at the moment and his mind was elsewhere. Steve did ask her if she needed to be escorted to her car, and she told him that Tony was handling that. Steve frowned and asked her if she was serious about this Tony guy. Korrine didn't feel comfortable talking to Steve about her relationship with Tony, so she smoothly changed the subject to something not so personal. Since that day, Steve hadn't been around much.

Korrine began to wonder if the note wasn't some bad joke, or maybe it had been put on her car by mistake. It wasn't addressed to her specifically, and she did have an ordinary car. It could've easily been a mistake. Korrine began to relax and forget about the note until one night at her studio her phone began to ring. She thought it was odd since it was after her listed work hours, and any specific client would just call her on her cell.

"Hello?" Korrine answered.

"Hello, is this Korrine?" the voice asked.

"This is she. May I help you?" Korrine simply stated.

"Did you get my note, Korrine?" Immediately, Korrine's heart began to beat with fear. "You never responded, and I see you still have that fucker hanging around. I told you that you needed higher standards. You need to take my advice." The caller disconnected before Korrine could respond.

Korrine didn't recognize the voice, and the number was unlisted. She shakily hung up the phone, and immediately called Tony. She was still shaking when he answered.

"Hey, sweetness, how's it going?" Tony asked in a cheery voice.

"Hey, Tony...uh...can you come to my studio, please?" Korrine responded nervously.

"Baby, what's wrong? Why do you sound like that?" Tony anxiously asked while grabbing his briefcase and keys, and heading out the door.

"I just received a phone call, and I'm scared," Korrine explained with a tear falling from her eye. Korrine angrily wiped the tear away. She was scared, but she was also angry. *Who in the hell thought they had the right to threaten her, and why?*

Tony drove like a bat out of hell, making a twenty-minute drive in half the time. He slammed his car door and stormed into Korrine's studio. He was furious. *Who in the fuck had the audacity to threaten his woman? There would be hell to pay!*

When he entered Korrine's studio, she was visibly shaking and wringing her hands. She ran and nearly jumped into his arms, and that just made Tony even more irate. He had never seen his sweetness like this before. This shit was going to end quickly. Korrine gave him a passionate kiss, and he wrapped her in his arms.

"Baby, it's okay. I'm here. No worries, okay?" Tony said in a soothing tone.

"I know, I'm just so...so....fuckin' mad!" Korrine shouted.

Tony backed up and looked at Korrine with half shock and half pride on his face. He knew Korrine wasn't a weak woman by any means, but he never expected her to be angry. "Sweetness, I thought you said you were afraid."

"I am, but I'm also pissed! Why is someone trying to make my life complicated? I'm finally happy, my career is going great, my creative juices are flowing, and I'm having the best sex of my *freakin'* life!" Korrine shouted as she paced back and forth.

Tony watched Korrine pace while ranting; he was both impressed and amused. He had never seen her *this* upset. It was really sexy, but there were more pressing matters to attend to.

Once Korrine calmed down, she called the detective she spoke to previously. She let him know about the call, but there really wasn't anything they could do since the call wasn't recorded and there wasn't a number listed. The officer advised her to record all of her future calls so that she could have proof she was being harassed.

After they finished talking to the police, Tony pulled Korrine into another tight hug and kissed the top of her head. She sighed and accepted his strength, even though she had her own; it was always nice to have someone else to lean on.

She'd been alone for so long that it was good to have someone to depend on, and she knew she could depend on Tony.

"So....let's talk about the 'best sex of your life' statement you made earlier," Tony said bringing Korrine out of her thoughts.

Korrine asked with a smirk, "When did I say that? I don't remember saying that."

"Oh yeah, sweetness. That's exactly what you said. I'm superman, remember?" Tony teased, pointing to himself.

"What does you being superman have to do with what you *think* I said?" Korrine asked amused.

"Superpowers include memory, and I definitely remember you saying 'best sex,'" Tony replied with a raised eyebrow.

"How can you think about sex at a time like this?" Korrine asked.

"Oh no you don't....*Yoooouuuu* brought up sex. I just remembered you saying it. Since you need to relax and calm down, let's get you home so I can give you what you need," Tony replied confidently.

Korrine and Tony went back to his place leaving her car at her studio. She thought of herself as a strong woman, but it just creeped her out that someone decided to mess with her in this way and she had no clue who it could be. It made her uneasy, and she didn't like to feel uneasy.

When they were at Tony's place, Korrine decided to call Lauryn and Brandon and let them know what was going on. Both were glad that she was with Tony, and that she wasn't alone. They were both equally worried, and they all decided to meet up that weekend to catch up on things.

After hanging up with Lauryn and Brandon, Korrine went in search of Tony. His place was way bigger than hers with a lot more rooms. She found him in his home office on the phone. When he saw her, he smiled his panty-dropping smile and ended the call.

"Hey, baby, I was just on the phone. A friend of mine can be over in two days to set up your office and cell with recording devices," Tony smiled.

Korrine smiled at him; he was so cute and sexy when he was being all protective.

"You know you are really sexy when you're being all protective," Korrine whispered seductively.

With that statement, the mood in the room changed from serious to seriously sexy in two seconds flat.

"Baby, you need to relax," Tony told Korrine as he grabbed her hand and sat her down on his desk.

It was very convenient that she was wearing a skirt. He slowly moved his hands up her thighs, working the skirt up along the way. She shivered under his touch, and he smiled at her reaction. He moved the tips of his fingers slowly up to tease her core. Korrine sighed and moved with the rhythm Tony was making with his fingers. She needed this; she needed him. She couldn't imagine being with anyone else at this moment. He was there when she needed him, in all the ways she needed him. *This is no fling; I'm falling for him. Shit! I AM FALLING FOR HIM! Shit! When did this happen?*

Korrine gasped out loud when Tony pushed his teasing fingers deep into her waiting center and began thrumming her clit. Korrine threw her head back in bliss. Her chest was rapidly moving up and down with each breath. She could feel her climax building, and then he stopped. *What the hell!?* Korrine looked up at Tony's smirking face. She narrowed her eyes at him when he slowly licked his fingers. He smiled, pushed her legs farther apart, and practically dove in. He licked and sucked on her clit, swirling his tongue and lapping up her juices until she was dry, and then making her wet all over again.

"Tony, baby, I can't take anymore," Korrine moaned.

Tony simply smirked and continued to lap at her essence.

"Baby, pleeeeeaaase," Korrine begged.

"I can't stop, baby. You taste so good," Tony responded to her pleas, refusing to stop.

"I think I'm going to pass out if you don't stop," Korrine whimpered.

Just then, Korrine's body tensed with her oncoming climax.

"Give it all to me damn it!" Tony growled.

He stuck his tongue deep inside her and began to sex her with his tongue. Korrine didn't know if she was coming or going. She was pulling and tugging at Tony's hair, but it only seemed to encourage him.

Her third orgasm hit her harder and more intense than the first two. Korrine was spent; all she wanted to do was sleep. Tony grinned down at Korrine, scooping her into his arms and carrying her to his bedroom. He undressed her and put her in bed. She sleepily looked at him and smiled. Korrine was fast asleep before Tony could finish getting undressed.

****

Korrine tried to wake Tony up early. She wanted to repay the favor; he made her orgasm three times and she fell asleep. She felt bad about that, so she decided to wake him up by licking around the head of his penis. She slowly caressed his balls all the while she was licking his shaft. She felt Tony began to slowly move, pumping himself up and down. She looked up, and his eyes were still closed. *He's still sleeping. I need to do better with my wake up calls.* Korrine put his entire penis in her mouth, sucking up and down. She licked up one side and down the other, gripping his shaft and moving her hand with precision. He began to moan, and she knew he was awake. He looked down at her through sleep-filled eyes, and he smiled his megawatt smile. Korrine began to really move, being turned on by the sounds Tony began to make. She knew he was close; his hips began thrusting at a frantic pace, and he grabbed her head pumping into her warm hot mouth. Korrine stayed perfectly still, opening her mouth wide while taking in all of him. She rubbed his balls with one hand while stroking his dick with the other. Tony got impossibly hard and went completely still while his cock drained into the back of her throat. Korrine licked her lips and Tony pulled her on top of him, kissing her before pulling the comforter over them and quickly falling back to sleep.

CHAPTER 10

Tony

Tony loved when Korrine woke him up like she did; her beautiful mouth and plumped lips were wrapped around his cock. *Ummmmm, I love that shit!* He couldn't believe his life. He could get used to waking up next to Korrine. He couldn't help but reach for her in the middle of the night; her curves and aroma that were all her own had him dazed. To know that she was in his bed had him with a feeling of contentment that he had never known. When she wasn't next to him in his bed, he felt incomplete. Four months ago he would have never even thought about waking up with a woman. In fact, he did his best never to spend the night with any woman; get in and get out, no sleepovers! But Korrine was worming her way into more than his bed; she had a place in his heart. He knew she wouldn't be just a fling, but the thought of a relationship was not Tony's style. How could one petite little woman play such a big part in flipping his world upside down? The thought of not having Korrine when he wanted—touching, kissing, licking her when and where he wanted—just wasn't something he wanted to comprehend. To think of anyone else having her was incomprehensible. He couldn't wait to make her his on a more permanent basis; he just needed to get her to trust him. However, there were a couple of problems. First, he had to make sure she knew that he was not a playboy, and he was serious about her. The biggest problem was that Korrine had a stalker; until he found out who the hell was stalking her, keeping her safe came before any wining and dining he may have done.

Tony couldn't believe that Korrine wasn't taking this stalker seriously. She continued getting the weird phone calls, but they weren't long enough to trace. Some were even coming from different computer IP addresses. She had a stalker for Christ's sake, and she had no idea who it could be. However, Tony had a solution to that problem; he was going to hire a private investigator. This shit was coming to an end, and he didn't care how stubborn she was; there was no way he was going to let this nonsense continue. Korrine tried to act tough, but he knew deep down she was afraid. After that first phone call, she was shaking like a leaf. She tried to say she was angry, and no doubt she was, but she was frightened too. He knew his sweetness, and he would protect her any way that he could; even if that meant her not knowing about the PI.

With everything that was going on with Korrine, Tony totally forgot about the dates or "booty calls" he had set up months before. His assistant Sarah called him on his office phone to let him know that Misty Austin, one of those many "dates" he forgot to cancel, was on her way up to his office.

Misty Austin was a beautiful blonde socialite. She had a rack you couldn't ignore (although they were clearly fake), legs that kept going and going, and beautiful crystal blue eyes. She was a dream to look at, but she was a gold digger if he had ever seen one. But she was an easy lay with pretty good head so Tony would entertain her from time to time.

Misty entered Tony's office in a huff. She was wearing a super tight, pink bandage dress that was entirely too short to be wearing anywhere but the bedroom. She was clearly upset about something, but Tony just really didn't care about what.

"Misty? What can I do for you?" Tony asked.

"What can you do for me? Are you serious, Tony? I have been calling you for weeks without even so much as a text in response. You have stood me up for three dates without even calling!" Misty practically screeched in a high-pitched voice that had Tony wincing.

"Misty, I've been entirely too busy to entertain you," Tony said dryly.

"Have you been busy with that black woman I've seen you with?" Misty accused Tony; narrowing her eyes.

Before he could answer her, Misty began ranting at Tony. She started pacing back and forth, waving her arms around frantically as her voice kept getting louder and louder.

"I can't believe you chose some black girl, some wannabe designer, over *me*. She clearly doesn't have the pedigree that I have; she can't complement you like I can. There is no way in hell she looks as good as me on her best day. What are you thinking? How will your parents respond to this girl? You can't take her to meet your father; he will have a heart attack! What you need to do, Antonio, is stop playing games with this girl and get you and me back on track. I'm tired of waiting for you to come to your senses!"

Tony just stared blankly at Misty for a minute. He couldn't believe the audacity of this woman to come to his office and question him.

"Who the *fuck* do you think you are?" Tony growled through clenched teeth.

Misty stepped back; the fury radiating from Tony was almost tangible. Misty hadn't noticed how angry Tony was during her rant, but now it couldn't be missed.

"I...uhhh...uhhh..." Misty stuttered, shocked by Tony's anger toward her. He had always been in total control, never showing much emotion toward her. He never even raised his voice at her. Although he wasn't shouting now, the look in his eyes and the cold chill in his voice made it unmistakable that Tony was indeed very, very angry. She took a deep breath, calming herself down, and took a step toward him.

"Tony, I came here to let you know that I'm not mad that you have been having some fling. But you blowing me off for some black girl is unacceptable, and you should know better. I'm the one you need to get serious with, not some ghetto hoe...some gutter trash with barely a career," Misty said with all the disgust she could muster.

Tony had to step back from Misty; he was looking at her in a whole new light. He knew she was vapid and shallow. Hell, he even knew she was a gold digger. She didn't care what he looked like or how he treated her, as long as the expensive dinners and the VIP treatment kept coming. Although he and Misty weren't ever an official item, she looked good on his arm at special events when he needed a date. He would take her out to dinner every once in a while. But mostly it was a hot quickie when he needed to get off and there was nobody else. He would call it friends with benefits, but he wouldn't necessarily call Misty a friend. She was barely an acquaintance…more of a bed warmer. Before he could talk to what was obviously a crazy person, Tony had to calm himself down. He would never put his hands on a woman in anger, but this bitch had lost her damn mind.

"I don't owe you an explanation. *Get the fuck out of my office*," Tony said this with a calm that was almost scary.

Misty shook her head in disbelief. "I'm leaving now, but know I will be back. I will give you a couple of days to calm down, and I will give you a call. And, Tony… you better fucking answer."

Tony couldn't believe the crazy that was coming from this woman. Had he been so caught up in her tits that he missed the crazy in her eyes? He knew she was hard up for cash these days. Her family's money was practically gone because her deadbeat father had gambled and swindled almost all of the money from their family business. They were living on favors and reputation. Misty knew she had to marry well, or she and her family weren't going to be able to keep up the charade for much longer.

"Get out, or I can call security. It's your choice," Tony demanded, dismissing Misty while holding open his office door for her to leave.

Misty took in a deep breath, narrowing her eyes. "Stay away from that girl!" Misty sashayed from the office as if it were hers with her head held high, her expensive purse in the crook of her arm, and her mouth formed in a perfect thin line. She thought she had won.

Tony was so livid that he was afraid of responding to Misty as she left his office. In fact, he was so upset at her impudence that he missed that she knew way more about Korrine than she should. Tony hadn't seen Misty in months, since before he started seeing Korrine, so she shouldn't know anything about her. However, Tony was so angry at the fact that this woman, who was essentially a bed warmer to him, tried to tell—no demand—that he do what she said. He couldn't think straight or see straight. He needed to calm down before he did something stupid, like chase after Misty and scare her away.

After his afternoon meeting with Misty, Tony decided to go work off some steam in his office gym before meeting with the PI about the logistics of the job he wanted him to perform. He also had the background information on Steve. He didn't trust that guy, and it wasn't because he was jealous. *Am I jealous of that guy?... Naaahhhh.* Tony couldn't think of himself as the jealous type. He knew his self-worth; hell, he was a catch. No, Tony didn't like Steve because of how he tried to push his way into Korrine's life. Every time he turned around, he was looking at Steve.

Steve McKinney was a smarmy bastard. Tony found out that he moved to Houston almost three years ago. His real estate business was doing pretty well, but he upped and moved to Houston for what seemed like no reason. But Tony had found the reason. Oh, Stevie boy had an estranged wife he was chasing. Seems like his wife had a new man, and Steve didn't like that much. He moved back to Dallas recently, but it looked like his wife had moved from Houston, not leaving much of a trail as to where she might have gone. Was she running from Steve and, if so, why? Steve had some skeletons in his closet concerning relationships, and Tony didn't like that one bit. Especially since Steve decided to pursue *his* woman, Tony knew that Steve was untrustworthy. But Korrine, being Korrine, only saw the good. That's what he loved about her...*Wait... Love?... Shit! Holy shit!*

He loved Korrine. But it had only been four months. He couldn't *love* her. No, he couldn't, but...he did.

DESIGNER DESIRES

CHAPTER 11

Tony

The realization of his love for Korrine was very confusing for Tony. In all of his thirty-four years, he had never been in love...lust definitely...but never love. Although he certainly lusted after Korrine and her luscious body, he knew that he loved her. He wasn't ready to admit that out loud yet; the notion was too scary. Besides, they hadn't even defined what they were doing. He would lightly bring up the subject of what they were, and she would lightly change the subject. Tony felt like the girl in all this, and the feeling was foreign to him. He needed to talk to someone—a man who could make heads or tails of "feelings."

Geez, he was definitely the girl.

"Jake, how have you been, man?" Tony asked his best friend and cousin.

"Hey, buddy. I'm good. How's it going? To what do I owe this rare occurrence?" Jake asked with obvious amusement.

"I met a woman..." Tony let his statement trail off, not knowing what to say next.

Jake chuckled. "Aww, a woman…it's about damn time."

"What? You act like I'm some virgin or something," Tony said slightly offended.

Jake chuckled again. "Come on, Tony. We both know you haven't been a virgin in what…two…three years now," Jake said laughing at his own joke. "I'm just stating the obvious; you have never been the type to call to 'talk' about a woman. Never!"

Tony sighed. "I know you know what type of man I am. I don't know how to deal with all these emotions and feelings and shit. This woman has me on edge, and I know I shouldn't be. But before I can stop myself, I'm saying and doing things I've never done before."

Jake laughed again. "Yeah, buddy, it's called love. No matter how much of an alpha male you might be, we all fall sometime."

Shit. Jake was right; Tony had fallen hard. He couldn't stop his growing feelings, no matter how he tried or what he did. He just resigned himself to the fact that he would have to do what he always did: take control of the situation.

"Yeah, I guess so. This feeling of not being in control is not something that I like. Anyways, this isn't just about this girly shit," Tony said changing the subject. "Korrine has a stalker, and we can't get a handle on who this fucker might be. I have some people on it, but I need family on this. Jake, she's important to me. I have to keep her safe."

"Oh, so Korrine is her name…nice," Jake replied with a smirk. Then he changed to a more serious tone void of his earlier amusement. "Okay, we will discuss the girly feelings and shit later. This stalker is serious, Tony. It's not often that *you* can't find information out. This guy must be real crafty."

Jake wasn't just Tony's best friend and cousin, he was also ex-military—special ops, to be exact—and he was the best in private security and investigations that Tony knew. When Tony thought of who could help him find Korrine's stalker, he knew only one person he would trust: Jake. However, Jake wasn't available. He was doing a special private security for some big client and was out of the country. Since Korrine hadn't had any physical contact with her stalker, Tony got a local guy to handle her case. But now that he was back, Tony wanted Jake's expertise.

"Yes, actually he is," Tony agreed. "Even my IT guru can't pinpoint the location these calls are coming from. All he found out was that it's some kind of computer program that switches IP addresses at random, so we know it's not coming from a cell or a landline but a computer. What we don't know is who or why."

Jake noted the worry in Tony's voice and said, "Well, gather all the details that you can and have Korrine available to speak to me. I will be there in two days at the latest. I would be there sooner, but I have to wrap up this last client and get my men in order. After that, I will be on the first thing smokin' to get to you and your girl."

"Thanks, man. I really appreciate your help," Tony sighed in relief for his cousin's help.

"Of course, man. It's always family first. You know that. I'll see ya in a couple of days. Oh and I can't wait to meet Korrine. I bet she's something if she's got you this torn up," Jake teased, the humor returning to his voice.

Tony smirked. "Oh man, you have absolutely no idea."

Once Tony disconnected from Jake, he felt lighter than he had in days. He knew Korrine could take care of herself, but he felt it was his job to protect her. He had an overwhelming need to make sure that she was safe and loved. *There's that damn word again...Uhhh...Why can't I get love off my brain? I have too much to do,* Tony thought.

Before he realized it, Tony was meeting with his last client of the day. He had a full day, and he still couldn't shake the feeling that stuck with him after the meeting with Misty and the phone conversation with Jake. Both conversations made him realize that maybe, just maybe, Korrine might be the one for him. It all just started out as fun, but with all the serious things going on with his sweetness, he couldn't help but get caught up in his feelings for this woman. It wasn't just about a quick roll in the hay or a beautiful woman to sate his needs. It was about knowing that this woman, who snuck up on him and found a place in his heart, needed to be safe. Tony would do any and everything he could to make sure that would happen.

Tony had a date with Korrine the next evening but, since he spent more than half his day either talking or thinking about her, he decided he would give her a call to see what she was up to. Even though his PI, George Anderson, had her under surveillance for the time being, he still needed to hear her voice.

The phone rang four times before Korrine picked up, seeming out of breath. "Hello?"

"Korrine? You okay, baby?" Tony asked.

"Hey, Tony. I'm fine. I was just finishing up a client, and I left my phone in the front of the studio. I had to run…you know, running is *not* my thing," Korrine explained chuckling.

Tony relaxed slightly. "Okay, I was wondering if you want to meet for drinks when you're done."

Korrine curiously asked, "Yeah sure, but I thought we had a date tomorrow. Are you canceling on me?"

"Nope, I just had a long day. Just wanted to see you is all," Tony replied.

"Are you doing ok?" Korrine asked a little concerned.

"I'm fine, sweetness. Are you almost done? Do you want me to swing by and get you?" Tony smiled.

"Sure, that way I can have a couple of drinks. I finished up my clients, so I actually have some time off for a couple of days before I have to start another design," Korrine stated happily.

"Good, I'll pick you up in thirty minutes?" Tony asked.

Korrine smiled. "Great, see ya then."

Exactly thirty minutes later, Tony pulled his white Range Rover up to Korrine's studio. He noticed that her car wasn't parked in her normal spot, but the lights were still on. So he hopped out of his truck and went to ring the bell. When he reached the door to her studio, it was ajar and he heard raised voices coming from inside. Tony paused when he heard a male voice. *Who the hell is that? And are they yelling?...At Korrine?...Wait a damn minute.*

Tony's steps quickened as he got closer to the voices. Not wanting to let his presence be known just yet, he walked quietly to see who the male voice was that was talking crazy to his girl. When he rounded the corner, he saw Steve standing entirely too close to Korrine. His stance was rigid and tense, and his fists were balled at his side. Tony didn't know what was going on, but Steve's demeanor alone had Tony wanting to whoop his ass.

"What the hell is going on?" Tony asked Steve with a menacing tone.

Steve instantly took a step back from Korrine, and she noticeably relaxed. However, neither said anything...which made Tony even angrier.

"I asked a question. What is going on?!" Tony asked again still looking at Steve.

Steve didn't answer, but Korrine did. "Steve was just leaving, Tony...Weren't you, Steve?"

Steve took another step back with his fists still clenched and his face turning redder. He turned around and narrowed his eyes at Tony. "Yeah, I was just leaving."

Steve left through a side door not having to pass Tony, which was good because Tony was ready to snatch this asshole up for talking to Korrine how he was. Although Tony didn't hear exactly what was being said, the tone he heard and the body language was enough.

Tony looked at Korrine with a raised eyebrow. She smiled a weak smile that didn't reach her eyes, and Tony instantly knew something was undoubtedly wrong.

"Sweetness...why was he yelling at you?" Tony asked.

"It was a misunderstanding, Tony...Nothing major. Steve just lost...I...he's been going through a lot lately," Korrine stuttered then smiled uncomfortably.

Tony stepped closer to her and spoke so seriously that Korrine shuttered. "Baby, let's get one thing straight. No man will yell at you in front of me or otherwise, and I will just let it go as a 'misunderstanding.' So although I'm very aware that you can take care of yourself, if you don't tell me what he was yelling about, I will catch that motherfucker and beat it out of him."

Korrine let out a sigh. "Really, Tony, it was a misunderstanding. He wasn't yelling. I wouldn't let anyone disrespect me, friend or not."

Tony didn't want to fight with Korrine, but he would catch Steve later. This was not the end of this shit. People were testing him lately, and he didn't like it one bit...not one little bit.

"Okay, sweetness, if you say it was a misunderstanding, then that's what it was. Just know that he better not *misunderstand* anything else with you using that tone," Tony replied.

"Fine, but it really isn't that serious…Okay?" Korrine tried to persuade him. "Just relax, and let's go get a drink. I really need one now."

Tony let it go for the time being. He didn't want to push the subject with Korrine, especially since he was going to ask Steve about it anyway. He smiled at Korrine, and went and wrapped his arms around her. He kissed her on the top of her head and breathed in her scent. She always smelled like some kind of fruit and lilac, with a bit of Korrine mixed in. It was intoxicating, and he couldn't get enough. She visibly relaxed in his embrace, and her arms went around his waist. She squeezed him gently and smiled up at him. When their eyes locked, Tony slowly lifted his hand and caressed Korrine's cheek. He leaned down and pressed his lips to hers. The kiss started out slow and gentle. But it quickly heated up, with the passion seeping in and making both Korrine and Tony want more. Tony stepped back, nipping Korrine's bottom lip but releasing her slowly. She whimpered at his departure, opening her eyes slowly.

She asked, "Why did you stop?"

He smirked, answering, "Because, sweetness, if we don't get going, we are going to be having sex in your studio."

She smiled and nodded. Korrine grabbed her purse, and they headed out to the local dive bar down the street from her studio.

When they reached his truck, he opened the door and let her in. He got into the driver's side and pulled out still looking for Korrine's car.

"Sweetness, where's your car?" Tony asked.

"I had to put it in the shop because of something with a light. I don't know..." Korrine trailed off.

Tony cut his eyes at her, not wanting to keep his eyes off the road for too long, "Something with a light? Did the mechanic tell you what it was?"

Korrine nodded. "Not yet. He's a friend of B's, so he won't cheat me. My bucket will last me a little longer. It's nothing serious, and it starts right up. I just wanted to get it checked out while I had some time off, and I didn't have to come to the studio for a couple of days."

"Okay, well that's reasonable. How did you get to work?"

"Brandon brought me. I was going to hitch a ride with Steve. But you called and I didn't need to...so..." Korrine stopped when she saw the look on Tony's face.

"What's the look for?" Korrine asked.

Tony was really trying not to argue with Korrine, but even the simple thought of Steve made his blood boil.

"Nothing, I just don't want you to have to depend on somebody like Steve," Tony said simply.

"Somebody like Steve? What does that mean?" Korrine asked starting to become annoyed.

"Somebody who *yells* at his friends. If you need something, Korrine, just let me know. I have extra cars; you can use whichever you want for however long you need to."

Korrine just stared at Tony's profile; she didn't want to fight with him, so she just let the comment go. She would have some drinks and go home to relax. If Tony acted like he had some sense, he could stay. But if he kept acting an ass, she would relax in a bath...alone.

CHAPTER 12

Tony

Tony didn't understand why Korrine was acting as if *he* did something wrong. He didn't do anything wrong. He just couldn't understand what her issue was. She kept defending that ass Steve and treating Tony like he was the one yelling at her. Whatever they were talking about before he interrupted them seemed to be more than a little heated. He could tell from Steve's body language that the conversation wasn't something he was enjoying, but Korrine just seemed uneasy— not scared, but uncomfortable. He really needed to know what was said. Steve was untrustworthy, and if he was upset at Korrine about something he needed to know. He would call his PI as soon as he could and get the comings and goings of Mr. Steve McKinney since he got back to Dallas. Korrine said he had a lot going on...so let's just find out what else Steve might be hiding.

Korrine and Tony lounged around the little bar around the corner from her apartment. They decided that it would be better to just go to her neighborhood instead of staying in Addison. They were trying to relax by sipping on cocktails, but the atmosphere just seemed off. It didn't seem like their usual easy going relaxed air when they were together. It wasn't tense, but it wasn't *them*.

Tony suddenly reached for Korrine's hand and rubbed small circles on her skin. She smiled at him shyly, and he let out a sigh.

"Korrine, I'm sorry about earlier. I just don't like *anyone* disrespecting you. But I get that Steve is your friend. Even if I don't particularly care for him, I respect you. Just don't be upset. I can't take this awkward silence between us. This isn't us," Tony said looking in Korrine's eyes.

Korrine smiled at Tony and relaxed. "I don't want to be mad, Tony. But you have to understand when I say it's nothing; you have to let it go, okay?"

Tony let out a breath. "Okay, sweetness. I get it."

The rest of the time at the bar was much more relaxed. They fell into the easy flow that they always had, and they laughed, talked, and touched each other in inappropriate places until neither could take anymore.

Tony threw a couple of bills on the bar and waved at the bartender as he grabbed Korrine's hand, pulling her towards the exit. *It seems I'm always dragging this woman out of a bar into my bed. I have got to control my hunger for her...eventually.*

****

Tony held Korrine's hand as they rode the elevator up to her uptown apartment. He wanted to pin her against the mirrored surface, yank her panties down, and slip deep within her warm, moist cavern. However, Korrine's little old neighbor lady from down the hall was in the elevator with them so he would have to wait to get his sweet Korrine pinned like he wanted her. Tony caught Korrine's gaze in the mirrored wall of the elevator; the twinkle of lust in her eyes made him smile, showing his dimples. She licked her lips in response, and her breath caught when he also licked his lips. The sexual tension was palpable. Even the little old lady looked between the two of them and smiled.

"You two make a lovely couple," the little old lady said with a wide smile.

Before Korrine could respond, Tony replied, "My girlfriend and I thank you very much."

Korrine narrowed her eyes at Tony, and he simply smiled and winked at her.

"In my day, you two wouldn't be able to love each other so freely the way you do. I'm glad things have changed." The little lady with gray hair, chocolate skin, and bright brown eyes smiled a wide smile and exited the elevator.

Both Korrine and Tony stood frozen for a moment, neither saying anything. How could a virtual stranger recognize what both of them were trying so hard to deny? They were clearly in love…and it showed.

The air between them turned awkward again for the second time that night. They slowly moved out of the elevator, not mentioning what the neighbor lady had said. They quietly walked to Korrine's apartment, both deep in their own thoughts. Korrine slowly opened the door, and both walked in as she turned on her lights.

Tony liked Korrine's apartment; it wasn't as big as his, but it definitely represented Korrine's free spirit. It was full of colors and homey décor. Tony's mind was wandering, trying to focus on anything except for the obvious elephant in the room. He just wasn't ready to admit that he was in love. He wanted Korrine to be his, but love was a level he wasn't sure of. Even though he knew what the woman spoke was nothing but the truth, he couldn't even say it to himself and for sure not to Korrine. He didn't have a clue as to what she thought about their relationship…if you could call it that. Hell, he didn't know what to call it, but the conversation had to be had. He couldn't go on this way.

Tony closed her door and locked it, walking to sit on her comfy overstuffed couch. "Korrine, can we talk?"

"Yeah, I think we need to," she agreed. "Would you like something to drink? Wine or scotch?"

"Scotch, please," Tony responded.

Korrine went to her kitchen, pouring Tony a scotch and herself a glass of Moscato. She came back into her family room and sat the drinks on her coffee table. She sat beside Tony and let out a long sigh. "Let's talk…"

CHAPTER 13

Korrine

The talk didn't go as Korrine expected. What she assumed would take place was the break-up talk. They've been living in a fantasy world these past few months. Korrine knew about Tony's playboy ways. She would never expect a commitment from him. Hell, she didn't want one; all she wanted was a good time and a roll in the sack to dust the cobwebs out. She never thought that she and Tony would have so much in common, or that she would feel so at ease with him. And then of course there was the pure sexual chemistry that she never would have expected them to have, but she was really, *really* glad that she found that out. She never would have expected out of all the surprises that the sex between them would be the biggest and the best. The raw sexual prowess Tony possessed was something that Korrine had never experienced. Her awareness of him was unbridled; she would practically shiver from just a look from him, and touching was a whole other subject. His touch drove her crazy. One simple sweep of a fingertip against her bare skin, and she was wet and ready.

Korrine started the conversation trying to give Tony an out of their situation; she wasn't sure you could call it a relationship, but she knew they had something. So she would call it their "situation" until they stopped ignoring the topic. However, Korrine wasn't ready just yet to talk about their status, but that's exactly what Tony wanted to talk to her about.

"Look, Korrine, I want to be exclusive," he said, holding her hand. "Just the thought of seeing you with someone else causes me an unfathomable amount of discomfort. I've never experienced this shit before in my life!"

The sight of this once playboy looking at her with so much sincerity, caused Korrine's heart to melt. Yet, she had to stick to her guns. "Tony, I think you may be overreacting. Like you said, you've never been in this situation before.

Maybe you're just uncomfortable because you're not getting exactly what you want when you want it."

Tony had a look of total exasperation on his face.

"I'm not dating anyone else, and I'm not planning on it," Korrine told him. "I just don't think I'm ready for a serious relationship right now. I'm busy with my career, and I don't want you to feel disregarded or neglected when I have an overload of work and I can't see you as much."

"Okay, we can take things slower if that's how you feel, Korrine, but, like I've told you before, I'm not into game playing. You are who I want, but if I have to take a step back and give you space I can do that," Tony responded disappointedly.

Tony wrapped Korrine in a body smothering hug, kissing her long and slow; caressing her tongue with his, leaving his mark on her as best he could. When he released her from his embrace, Korrine was panting and wanting like never before.

Tony left that night without him and Korrine making love. It was the first time since they had been together.

Korrine thought maybe it was just about his ego, but the sincerity in his voice and eyes when he told her how he felt said that he was actually telling the truth. *But can I trust him?*

Korrine was a little more than afraid to take that step with Tony. Even though she hadn't been dating anyone else, just to have that option gave her a sense of comfort. She knew how she felt about him, but she wasn't ready to give her heart to another man—especially one that was known to have a horde of women at all times. No, she wouldn't be cheated on or be a part of anyone's harem. She wanted something real this time, and she would guard her heart.

It had been a week since Tony and Korrine's conversation, and she still didn't have any clue as to why she just couldn't commit to him. She was simply going through the motions at work. Finishing up old designs and starting new ones didn't give her the peace she came to know from designing. All she could do was think about Tony and how he treated her. He had shown her nothing but attention and affection. Even when they went out together, he acted as if she was the only woman in the room. But Korrine had to ask herself. *How long would it last? Would he get bored and cheat? Did he want to control the situation? Am I just hurting his ego by not saying he's my one and only?* The questions kept coming, making Korrine more and more confused. She had to stop! She needed a girl's night to clear her thoughts and anxieties.

Korrine called Brandon and Lauryn to meet her at The Porch, a restaurant near her apartment, since her car was still in the shop. An hour later, Korrine, Brandon, and Lauryn were at the restaurant laughing, talking, and genuinely having a good time when Brandon brought up the elephant in the room.

"Korri, what's going on with you, baby girl?"

Korrine sighed and shrugged. Both Brandon and Lauryn looked at her with pity in their eyes and small smiles on their faces.

"Guys, I just don't know what to do. Tony and I have been having a great time together. He has been the fun that I've been missing, but it scares me that he's asking to be exclusive. He's never been the type. You know?"

"Korri, I know. I'm biased because Tony is my cousin, but he really is a great guy," Lauryn said.

"I'm not disputing that he's a good guy, Lo. I'm just not sure he can be exclusive. You know more than anybody how many women Tony has at his beck and call."

"Yeah, but just because women want him doesn't mean he will just cheat on you, Korri," Brandon stated.

"Korri, women have always thrown themselves at my cousin; he's a good-looking guy with a lot going for him. But even with all the women he may have had around, he is not a cheater. Those women all knew what was going on. They all wanted a chance to change him or be the one. He never led any of them to think that they were more than what they were."

"I don't think that makes me feel any better," Korrine replied dryly.

"It should," Lauryn stated simply. "Not once did he want to be exclusive until you."

"I know he's your cousin, but you seem to know an awful lot," Korrine responded with a raised eyebrow.

"These women try to befriend me to get closer to the men in my family. Tony is not my only hot cousin. They reveal more to me than they should," Lauryn said with a smirk.

Korrine sighed. "I see."

"You're thinking too much, baby girl," Brandon told her. "Tony helps you have fun, and you said yourself that you are more creative. You're definitely more relaxed. For once stop being so damn guarded and go for your happiness. Every man isn't that fucktard Darren."

Both Korrine and Lauryn burst out laughing. "Fucktard? B, where did you get that from?"

"Brent," Brandon smiled.

"Oh, good. Let's talk about somebody else's love life, because I'm exhausted talking about mine." Korrine smiled.

"Oh no, this girls' night is about you and your man. There is no need to start discussing my business because I'm good," Brandon said.

Korrine sighed again. "Look, I get what you all are saying; I hear you loud and clear. Bad habits are hard to break, and guarding a broken heart is hard not to do. But I promise I will try. So let's drink up and have some fun tonight, okay?"

The three friends ate and drank until the restaurant was closing. They all had more to drink than they planned, so they walked back to Korrine's apartment still laughing and cutting up. When they reached Korrine's apartment, Tony was leaning against the door with his hands in his pockets. They all stopped mid stride, and all conversation stopped. Korrine was more than a little surprised. They hadn't seen each other for a week, and she didn't realize until that moment how much she truly missed him.

Korrine examined Tony from head to toe. He was pure masculinity with his dark wash jeans that were a perfect fit over his thick thighs and his blue button down shirt that was a slim cut. He had it rolled up at the elbows with two buttons undone so that it stretched across his broad chest with the material straining over his massive biceps. His face had a little stubble, and his hair was tousled. When their eyes met, he smirked.

Yep, I've just been caught checking him out.

They both smiled, and Korrine felt her face heat with embarrassment. She slowly walked to him, forgetting about Lo and B. He visibly relaxed as she came to stand directly in front of him. Tony looked at her slightly bending down, and Korrine tip toed to meet him half way. Their lips locked in a sweet, gentle kiss...a kiss that said "I miss you," and "I'm glad you're here." Her arms circled his neck, and his went around her waist; picking her up as he stood up straight. She wrapped her legs around him and deepened the kiss. Tony moaned, and that's when they heard the clapping and hollering from their audience.

Tony slowly put Korrine back on her feet and gave her one last kiss on her plump lips before releasing her and turning his attention to the two idiots making too much noise. Korrine also turned her attention to her friends while trying to compose herself enough to chastise them. *It has only been a week. Calm down, Korrine. You nearly stripped this man's clothes off in the hall in front of your friends. Control yourself.*

"Okay, let's all go in. There's no need for us to be out in the hall putting on a show any longer," Korrine said as she blushed.

Korrine unlocked her door and they all followed behind her. Lo and B were clearly tipsy, so they headed straight for her overstuffed couches—flopping down as if exhausted—while Korrine and Tony slipped into her bedroom.

"Hey," Korrine said to Tony once they were inside her bedroom with the door locked.

"Hey," he replied.

"I missed you," Korrine said shyly.

"I missed you." Tony smiled walking closer to her.

"I know I said I would give you some time but, like I said, I missed you," Tony stated, making lazy circles with his fingers on her thigh.

Korrine couldn't think with him touching her, but she didn't need to think anymore. She was tired of thinking; she was going to take B's advice and go for her happiness.

"I don't need any more time. I know what I want."

"Oh," he replied with a raised eyebrow. "And what's that, Ms. Taylor?"

"You."

"You have me already."

"You, *exclusively*," Korrine said with a smile.

Tony leaned over and kissed Korrine with more passion than she had ever felt in her life. If she wasn't already sitting down, her knees would have buckled under the heat she was feeling. He groaned into her mouth, and she let out a sigh of contentment. The two of them made up for the week they spent without each other. They tried being quiet, knowing they weren't in the apartment alone but failed miserably. Korrine could not hold back her moans and screams if someone paid her to, and it was Tony's mission to make sure she knew that she was his...finally. He didn't give a damn who heard.

Korrine knew she would never be the same. Although they had sex many, many times before, this time was different. This time meant more than just sex. This time was the beginning of something she said she wasn't looking for but ultimately found anyway.

****

The next morning Korrine woke from a deep, restful sleep. She knew why she felt so relaxed. It was because of the big tank of a man that had her pinned to the mattress again. Anytime they slept together, Korrine would wake up with Tony wrapped around her. However, now she didn't mind. Tony grumbled and pulled her closer to him. She giggled and squirmed in his tightened embrace.

In a sleep filled voice, Tony asked her, "Mornin', sweetness. Did you sleep well?"

"Yes, superman, I did, but I need a drink of water, so you need to let me get out of this bed," Korrine replied with a giggle.

Tony kissed the top of her head and let her get up.

When she crept into the kitchen to get some water, she was met with a set of smirking faces. Both Brandon and Lauryn had passed out in the family room, but neither were drunk enough to miss the incredibly loud make-up sex that Korrine and Tony had.

Korrine felt the heat rise to her face as she said, "Good morning."

They replied in unison, "GOOOOD MOOORNINIG TO YOU TOO!"

They all laughed, and Korrine finished getting her drink before heading back to her room to a waiting Tony. She knew she couldn't be quiet, so she would settle for cuddling with him until the two intruders went home. She would give them a couple of hours before they had to go. She and Tony had some making up to do. And if it was anything like the night before, they were going to be making up for the rest of the day.

CHAPTER 14

Korrine

Every day since she made up with Tony, things had been blissful for Korrine. They were spending time together as a couple, not just in the bedroom, but in public. They would normally go on dates, but this time it was different. The atmosphere was more romantic, neither of them feeling unsure of what was happening between them and just going with the flow. Korrine never thought confessing that she indeed wanted to be exclusive with Tony would give her such peace and be so easy. She was so fearful that her memories of Darren would ruin any commitment with another man, she was pushing relationships away without even recognizing it.

They spent so much time together that Korrine had practically moved in with Tony. If they weren't working, they were together. And with each passing day, they became closer. Even though it was bringing her a great deal of peace to be with Tony, whenever they weren't together, she couldn't help the nagging doubts that would creep in her mind. *What if it ends? What if he tires of me? What if he starts resenting the fact that I work so much? What if...What if....What if...*

But in spite of all her doubts, she couldn't control her heart or her growing feelings. They were passionate and raw with each other. It was so different from anything she had ever experienced before. Although Korrine couldn't keep her mind from questioning her relationship and her feelings, her work hadn't suffered as she feared. Another one of her designs was a big hit on the red carpet, thanks to the pop star Tia, and she was in more demand than she could've ever hoped for.

With all the new and great things that were going on in her life, her biggest problem was that she was still getting crazy phone calls and there had been several more notes left at her studio. Korrine was set to have a meeting with Tony's cousin Jake to help find the person responsible for the threats. Korrine wasn't too happy with Tony once she found out he had hired a private investigator without speaking with her first, but it wasn't like he was following her. He was just looking into the traces that were placed on her phones. Since Korrine already knew about the phone taps, she thought it was necessary that Tony had someone look over them. It still bothered her a little that he hired someone without speaking to her; sometimes his over protectiveness was over the top.

But he was only looking out for me....right? Korrine thought.

Korrine met Jake at Tony's office later that day. She could definitely tell the two were related. Both men were built very similar. Both stood at around 6'5", although Jake may have been slightly taller. And he had more bulk than Tony, if that was possible. Korrine couldn't fathom that until she laid eyes on Jake. Where Tony had chocolate hair and eyes, Jake had blond hair and bright green eyes. He also had the signature Cameron dimples. Korrine did her best not to swoon when she laid eyes on the two finest men she had ever come across.

Korrine stepped into Tony's office with a wide, bright smile putting her own dimples on display. When the two men noticed she was there, they both stood to greet her. Both of them had bright smiles, but Tony had that wicked twinkle in his eye that he always had when he saw her. He slowly looked her up and down, perusing her body. Korrine wore a sleeveless purple maxi dress that hugged her body in all the right places. It was a tank top, so it showed just the right amount of cleavage. The purple fabric clung to her ample behind and flared out at the bottom. She paired the dress with a jean jacket and gold jewelry; a necklace that hung alluringly between her breast, and matching gold bangles with a pair of sandals. Her hair was down hanging around her shoulders in jet black soft beach waves.

"Hello, gentlemen. How are you guys?" Korrine greeted them brightly. "You must be Jake. I'm Korrine Taylor," she said extending her hand.

Jake smiled his dimpled smile and took Korrine's hand in a firm shake. "Yes, I'm Jake. It's nice to finally meet you, Korrine. I've heard *a lot* about you."

Korrine felt her face heat, and she smiled a shyly while still shaking Jake's hand. Tony walked around his desk and slowly took Korrine's hand from Jake's.

"Enough holding my woman's hand. Get your own," he told Jake jokingly while pulling Korrine into an embrace. Jake chuckled at his cousin; he couldn't believe that Tony found a woman he would actually feel possessive over. Even though Jake knew Tony was joking, he saw the way he looked at Korrine. He was clearly in love.

Korrine tiptoed to reach Tony's lips for a swift hello kiss, but he wasn't having it. Tony pulled her tighter against him, wrapping his arms around her and deepening the kiss. She gasped at the contact, and Tony took the opportunity to slip his tongue in her mouth to deepen the kiss even more. It was the two of them in their own little world. When Korrine heard herself groan, she knew she was completely lost in him...until she heard a throat clearing and a slight chuckle.

Korrine felt the heat rise to her face for the second time since she got there, and she slowly pulled away from Tony. He reluctantly moaned a little and let her pull away. He looked down at her, smirked and winked before addressing his cousin.

"Buzzkill," Tony said to Jake while leading them to the leather sofa in his office so they could get more comfortable.

Jake chuckled again, and Korrine's face heated even more. She was completely embarrassed that she let Tony kiss her like that in front of his family which she just met. She would always lose herself in his kisses, and she was throbbing and ready to jump his bones right there, cousin or not, and he knew it too.

Tony gave Korrine a knowing look and licked his lips.

Arrogant ass.

"Okay, you two. Let's get this show on the road before I see more of you than I'm willing to see; not that I would mind seeing you, beautiful...But this lunkhead?... No thanks," Jake teased with a smirk.

Tony smirked at his cousin and then at Korrine, who was still blushing. The meeting was going smoothly, with Korrine giving Jake copies of the notes that were left at her studio; the police had the originals. She told him that there wasn't anyone in her past that she could think of that would want to stalk her. She also told him about her ex Darren, but thought he wasn't a possibility because she hadn't seen or spoken to him in two years. She just didn't have a clue. While she and Jake were talking, Tony received a phone call and excused himself from the room. Jake took the opportunity to see how Korrine was really feeling about her stalker without Tony's presence.

"Korrine, how are you really feeling? I've been in private security for over a decade now, and I know how to read people. I can tell you aren't as calm as you're trying to portray."

Korrine took a deep breath and nervously looked at the door that Tony was standing outside of. "I'm trying to stay calm. But you're right, I'm a wreck. I have absolutely no idea who is doing this or why it is happening to me. It scares me to death. Obviously this is some crazy person. I don't have any experience with this sort of thing."

Jake nodded in understanding. "I get it. So here is one last question. Have there been any new people in your life lately?"

"Uh…no…not rea-" Korrine didn't finish before Tony cut her off as he returned to the office.

"Steve," Tony said with conviction.

"Steve isn't a new person in my life. I've known Steve for years," Korrine said.

"You haven't *known* Steve for years, Korrine. You haven't seen him in the last two years. He just showed up a couple of months ago, and since he's been here, the stalking started."

"Steve *is not* stalking me, Tony!" Korrine insisted through clenched teeth while narrowing her eyes at him.

Tony narrowed his eyes at Korrine in return. "You don't know *who* is stalking you, and Steve is just as good a candidate as anyone."

"With that type of thinking, *you* could be stalking me!" Korrine shouted.

Jake cut in before Tony could respond. "Okay, guys. Look, this is a tense situation. Emotions are high, and yelling at each other is not going to get us any closer to the person who is causing all this nonsense. Korrine, I understand that this Steve person is your friend. But technically he is new to the fold, and I need to check him out."

Korrine crossed her arms over her chest and huffed in deep breaths in exasperation. "I know you guys are trying to help, and I don't want to seem ungrateful. But you can't just go around accusing people of stalking because you're jealous." Korrine looked directly at Tony when she said the last part.

Tony then took the same stance, crossing his arms over his chest. "I'm not jealous of anybody. I'm only trying to protect you, and you do sound ungrateful."

Korrine stood slowly to her feet, and looked over at Jake. "It was nice meeting you. Jake, if you need anything else from me, *you* are welcome to call anytime." Korrine never looked at Tony as she grabbed her purse and sauntered through the door.

Jake looked at Tony, shaking his head with a smirk on his face. Tony, on the other hand, was furious and was scowling at the closed door.

****

Korrine couldn't believe the audacity of Tony. He called her ungrateful just because she didn't agree with him. *Asshole! I knew he liked control. But I didn't know it would go so far as, if I disagreed with him, for him to call me names. Asshole! I am not ungrateful! He's just jealous! We just got over our last fight; will it always be this hard? Is this even worth it? Why am I questioning myself again?! Uh...I need a drink...*

Korrine finally stopped pacing her apartment long enough to pour herself a glass of wine. She wanted something stronger, but it was only Tuesday. Although she had a light week, she didn't want to have a hangover in the middle of it. She just couldn't understand why Tony had such a low opinion of Steve. Besides the awkward encounter at her studio a couple of weeks back, she saw no real reason why Tony would have ill will towards Steve.

Yet, she had to admit that the argument with her and Steve *had* been pretty bad before Tony got there.

"Korri, why are you avoiding me? I thought we were friends? Every time I turn around, you are blowing me off for someone you claim you're not even dating. So what's really going on with you two?" Steve questioned Korrine his face *slightly red with aggravation.*

"I haven't been avoiding you, Steve. I've just been busy, that's all," Korri responded with a questioning look.

"You see how late I'm here working; you work just as much as I do. Otherwise, you wouldn't be here to walk me out so often," Korrine told Steve still not understanding why he was questioning her in this way.

"Korri, it's not just work and you know it. I see that Tony guy here all the time, and I don't see you turning him down to

go to lunch or dinner, or to just hang out with me. I mean, we are friends just like you two are, right?" Steve questioned again.

"Look, Steve, my situation with Tony really isn't any of your business," Korrine stated simply. "I haven't stood you up or even rescheduled anything. When I can't go hang out with you, I let you know up front...and you know it. What I do with Tony has nothing to do with what I do with you."

"None of my business...of course it's my business! You have been leading me on and you know it, Korri. You know I like you as more than a friend."

"Steve, you have the wrong idea. I had no idea that you wanted more than friendship. That's all I can offer at the moment. You're a nice guy, and I hope we can remain friends," Korrine said with a small smile on her face.

Steve looked angry. His face was beginning to turn red, and his fists were balled at his sides. He took a step toward Korrine, narrowing his eyes. "Korri, I don't understand why we have to be friends. We could be good together."

Korrine backed up a little looking at Steve. "Steve, you don't seem like yourself... Are you okay? This can't be about me."

Steve took a step back and took a deep breath. His face was still red, and his fists were still balled at his sides. But he seemed calmer. "I'm sorry, Korri. It's not about you. You're right; I'm just stressed out. I needed your friendship tonight, and you called and canceled. I guess I'm just having a really bad da..."

Tony walked in before Steve could finish his sentence.

Damn, I forgot how intense that conversation was, Korrine thought. *I was so focused on calming Tony down that I forgot all about the exact words Steve was saying to me. He wanted more, and he thought I was leading him on...Shit maybe my stalker is Steve!*

CHAPTER 15

Tony

*Every time we take two steps forward, we take three steps back. I don't understand why Korrine insists on fighting with me. I'm completely right about this. Steve is the most viable suspect. He's pushing his way into Korrine's life. His office is right next to hers. He made it seem like a lucky coincidence, when my PI George told me he was in a bidding war and virtually paid twice as much for the building when there was a cheaper location that he already had a bid on that he withdrew after learning about the occupants of the building next door, i.e., Korrine. However, I can't tell Korrine any of this without letting her know that I had George investigating Steve long before she received any calls. Shit....*Tony was brought out of his thoughts when his assistant Amanda knocked on the door.

"Boss, Mr. Diaz is here to see you. Should I send him in?" Amanda inquired.

Brian Diaz was looking for a new agent. After the current MLB season, he was going to be a free agent.

"Yes, Amanda. Send him in," Tony answered while standing. He was happy for the distraction. His thoughts had been on Korrine since their fight the day before. Tony felt uneasy not being with her, but knowing she had security helped him feel better. Of course, she didn't know about Jake's guys keeping a watchful eye on her. But what she didn't know wouldn't hurt her. He would keep her safe from a distance.

Once the meeting with Brian was concluded, Amanda stuck her head in the door and told Tony that he had several "urgent" messages. Tony was instantly on alert; did something happen to Korrine? Did Steve finally get to her? What was going on, and why didn't Amanda interrupt the meeting if it was urgent? Tony's thoughts were racing; not having control over this situation with Korrine was weighing heavily on him. All he wanted to do was protect her and make her his, but she just wouldn't let him. She kept her guard up so high; he couldn't imagine ever breaking through.

Amanda walked timidly through the door handing him the messages. Amanda's behavior was odd. She was always confident, and she was also one of the few people that could handle Tony. With his controlling nature and stubborn persistence of always being right, he was a hard man to please. Amanda usually took it all in stride, but today was different.

"Amanda? Who are the messages from?"

"Several are from Ms. Austin. She is very persistent and insists that you call her immediately-" Amanda said the last part while rolling her eyes.

"Okay, calls from Misty aren't something I would consider urgent," Tony stated.

"Those aren't really the calls that were marked 'urgent' boss. I was just stalling really...Ummm...Sir, your father called. He said he was coming into town, and he needed to inform you of the time and place to meet him for dinner."

Tony took a deep breath while clenching and unclenching his fists. He was trying to remain calm. His father was the last person he wanted to see. The last thing he needed was hounding about the family business again. His father was upset that Tony had no real interest in the "family" business. After he set out on his own, his father couldn't bear the idea that Tony would not be under his thumb and not easily controlled like the rest of his family...well, except for Jake. Tony refused to go into the business when he was twenty-two and straight out of college, and he definitely wouldn't be doing it now at thirty-four. Anderson Cameron was a force; he was from the old school and ran his family with an iron fist and a closed heart. He was a ruthless businessman who took lots of risks and shortcuts to get where he was. He felt like "hard work" was for fools who didn't know how to use the resources that were available. He took over the "family" business from his father after the old man keeled over. Anderson never cared too much for his own father. He thought he was too soft, and he had the power and control that Anderson longed to have. It took years and a lot of underhanded dealings to get full control of the Cameron Empire. But the old man did have a sense of tradition, and he built the Cameron name to be legendary. Anderson Cameron made sure his family never forgot what having that name entailed. It was his way and no other. He never accepted Tony's career path, although he was highly successful and one of the highest paid agents in his field with the number one firm in the U.S.

Tony's company had an emerging international clientele, expanding into all types of sports, from the NFL, NBA, MLB, to the Premier league in soccer, and even some Formula 1 drivers. Not to mention he was a millionaire ten times over. But his father wasn't proud of his son for venturing out on his own and becoming a success. No, he was resentful that he walked away from what Anderson considered his family obligations. Tony wasn't easily controlled or manipulated like his mother. He had a strong will that wasn't easily broken, but Anderson was trying to remedy that.

"When and where would my father like to meet?" Tony asked Amanda finally finding his calm.

"He wants to meet at the Reunion Tower at the Five Sixty restaurant tonight at 8pm," Amanda responded.

"Thank you, Amanda," Tony replied in a huff.

Amanda nodded and turned to leave.

Tony hated when his father came to town, but he definitely didn't need the distraction with everything that was going on with Korrine right now. Even though it had only been a couple of months, he felt a connection to her that he never felt before. Tony couldn't get her off his mind, no matter how many times they argued. She was completely stubborn. This wouldn't be the last argument they had, if he had anything to say about it that is. But now he couldn't even focus on getting her to see that she was being completely unreasonable and to make up with him. It hadn't been a full twenty-four hours, and he missed her plump lips that seemed to always be in a permanent pout. No, he wouldn't be able to focus on Korrine until his father was back in Georgia.

Kasey Martin

CHAPTER 16

Tony

Tony walked into the restaurant breathing slowly, trying to relax before seeing his father. He knew that the conversation was going to be the same as always; his father trying to control him by using his money and business, and Tony trying to control himself from punching his father in his smug face. This would be a long and excruciating night, and he didn't even have Korrine to get lost in once he was done with this mess....He would have to rectify that soon. Maybe even tonight.

"Antonio, have a seat, son," Anderson Cameron said as Tony approached the private table in the back of the restaurant.

"Father, to what do I owe this unexpected visit?" Tony questioned.

"I've gotten some astonishing calls from some...shall I say friends...who have stated that you have gotten mixed up with some gal, and she has you in all sorts of trouble."

Gal? What the fuck? Is this Gone with the Wind? I really can't stand this bastard.

Tony didn't respond. He sat looking at his father with a cold chill in his eyes. His father took that as a sign of agreement and started to go in for the kill.

"It's time that you stop with this foolishness. You are bringing shame to the Cameron name running around with all types like some miscreant. You've wasted a lot of time. You should have a wife and a family by now, son. This is not how I raised you; laying down with some girl with no family name…and she's black!" Anderson shook his head in disgust before continuing. "The least you could do is date someone of your own pedigree; you can't afford to run around with some nobody. What if she gets pregnant? You want to have some illegitimate child who is half black?!!" His father whispered the last part, not because of the unspeakable racism that flowed freely from his lips, but because he was scared someone would hear his son was sleeping with a black woman. Anderson stopped talking to take a sip of his scotch.

Tony sat across the table from the old man, seething with rage, but not wanting to give his father the satisfaction he was obviously seeking from getting Tony riled up. Tony took calming breaths and looked at his father. He sat watching Tony, seemingly waiting for him to fly off the handle.

Tony sat back in his chair, regaining his control, and spoke in a steady voice filled with warning. "Father, I am my own man. You have no say so in my life. Period. So, why are you here?"

Anderson leaned up, addressing Tony eye to eye. "You have responsibilities to uphold the family name. First, you run off so you wouldn't have to be responsible for your part in the family business, but you refuse to give up your shares. Secondly, you have a vested interest by continuing to keep those shares, but you refuse to be involved with your own family." Anderson's voice started to rise as he continued. "Lastly, you keep gallivanting around with these worthless whores who only want you for your money, all the while bringing shame on the family! Do you know your mother would die if she knew?"

Tony sat shocked by the pure hatred radiating off his father. How could this man have had a part in creating him? The ignorance was unbelievable, and his rage was at a boiling point.

Anderson narrowed his eyes. "What will it take to get you to open your eyes, son? This new gal you've been running around with is nothing but some whore trying to get into your pockets. I taught you better than that. You don't date the help, son; you fuck them and leave them where they are."

Tony couldn't hold the rage any longer. Not only had he insulted him and the woman that he was in love with, but he also had the audacity to be serious. Tony gave his father the iciest look he had ever given a man. "You don't have fuck all to say to me about my life. You don't know shit about me, old man. I don't know what you think you know about my love life, but I can tell you that you don't know shit about that either. What I suggest you do is to get on a plane and take your bigoted ass back to Georgia before I do something that both of us will regret."

Tony stood and pushed his chair out so hard that it nearly toppled over. He marched from the restaurant seething, but never looked back at his father. If he did, he was afraid that he would kill the old bastard right there where he sat.

Anderson Cameron was surprised by Antonio's will power. He was sure that mentioning his latest whore would get him to make a scene and get him right where he wanted him. But Antonio said what he thought would be the ending to the conversation, and simply walked away. But this wasn't the last of this conversation. He knew that he and the girl hadn't talked in the last day or so, and he thought this little fling of his son's was over. But, seeing Tony's reaction, he now knew that this girl was more of a distraction than he thought. Antonio was stubborn, but he would have to come around to seeing things the Cameron way; which is the way that Anderson needed things to be done. The girl had to go...once and for all.

"I just met with my son. It's as bad as you said," Anderson spoke into his cell.

"He is refusing to take my calls, and I've been to his office only to be refused entry," Misty responded. "I don't know what she has, but your son won't walk away from this one. If we're going to get him to marry me—hell, at this point, even just sleep with me—I need access to him. That's something I don't have at the moment."

"I thought you said this girl was taken care of."

"I thought she was. But he just won't stay away from her, even though she's clearly more trouble than she's worth. He just keeps going back for more," Misty stated, getting angrier the more she talked about Korrine.

"You said the guy you had was all too willing to take care of our little distraction. So what the hell is this guy doing?" Anderson asked in frustration.

"Well, he doesn't seem to be getting anywhere with her. So maybe we need to step up the game plan. We only have a short time remaining before all hell breaks loose. We need Tony's shares in the company, or you and my father are going away for the rest of your lives."

"I told your dumb ass not to talk about the situation over the phone, you stupid girl," Anderson spat into the phone. "Just do what needs to be done." Then he disconnected the call.

Misty looked at her phone enraged. She was not a stupid girl. *I am a very intelligent woman, and all you Camerons are soon going to find that out.*

Misty sat seething in anger. Her father and Anderson had dragged her into some bullshit, and she messed around and actually caught feelings for Tony. She had to work another angle if she was going to get Tony back where she needed him to be.

DESIGNER DESIRES

CHAPTER 17

Tony

Tony was pacing back and forth in front of Reunion Tower waiting for the valet. He kept replaying the conversation with his father in his head. He knew too much about his life and dealings with Korrine. Why was he interested in Tony's shares? Something was amiss.

He dialed Jake's number. He was missing something, and he needed to connect the dots and quick.

"Hey, buddy. What's up?" Jake questioned after picking up on the first ring.

"A whole lot, cousin. It's some shit going on that I'm unaware of, and I need to find out ASAP what the hell it is," Tony replied.

"Sounds serious. My guys just gave me an update on Korrine, so it couldn't be her. She just left her studio and was headed to her apartment. So what's the new development?" Jake asked.

"My father. That bastard is up to no good. I can feel it, and this time I'm determined to find out what. Meet me at my place in twenty, and I will give you the information you need. In the meantime, I will get started with my own search."

"Will do. See ya in twenty," Jake responded hanging up.

Tony's mind was racing. Everything wasn't adding up, and he couldn't figure out why. There were missing pieces everywhere. Why was his father here from Georgia, asking questions about his dating life all of a sudden? His father never gave a flying flip about whom he dated in the past. He never even cared enough to know who or when he was dating anyone. Tony always knew that his father was a bigot, though. That was a well-known fact...something his father never tried to hide. Even though he was a well-known businessman, he was still a white man in the south and some things will never change. That was one of the reasons Tony left his family behind. He loved his mother and cousins. But, like Jake, he had to get away from them. Their outdated traditions and family money was suffocating him, and he ran fast and far to get away from them. First, he went to college in California on a football scholarship. He didn't want his father's money anywhere near his education. He knew that if he chose to let him pay for his college, he would try to control his major and try to make him go into the family business.

The family owned an investment company and real estate all over Georgia. It was the investment firm that made the money though. Anderson was acting president and CEO of the investment and financial sectors of the business, with his younger brothers Luke, Lauryn's father, and Jack, Jake's father, running different parts of the real estate portion of the company. Recently, the investment side of the business had been taking a loss. Like most investments, there were risks involved, but Anderson seemed to be taking bigger and bigger risks. However, in the last year, the turnaround in the business had been positive...miraculous even. Anderson had been hiding some dealings from his family, and his excuses for the sudden turnaround into the positive weren't adding up. But since Anderson was the oldest and had the most shares, that meant he had the power in the company. So nobody said anything. The family had more money than they would ever need, so nobody asked any questions. Tony wasn't any better; he never asked questions because he didn't want to be involved with his father or his business. But now it was time for the questions to be asked and the answers to be given.

A half an hour later, Jake and Tony were at his place going over the most recent happenings involving Tony's father. Tony grabbed a bottle of water from the fridge and sat in his leather recliner. Jake sat on the sofa with a computer on his lap and several different documents spread on the coffee table.

"Okay, so all of a sudden dear old uncle is here from Georgia asking questions about Korrine?" Jake asked with his brow furrowed.

"Not really asking questions…more like accusing me of ruining the family name by dating Korrine. He acted as if he knew everything there was to know; he even mentioned the 'trouble' she had gotten into."

"Now how would he know about Korrine's stalker and why?" Jake asked more to himself.

"Exactly. Something else he said reminded me of a conversation I had recently with Misty Austin. Both of them mentioned having the right pedigree."

Jake snorted. "What are you? A damn show dog?"

Tony narrowed his eyes at his cousin. "Their words not mine, but it is unusual that they both used the same wording is all; that's just too much of a coincidence. Anyway, at first I didn't pay much attention to Misty. She's just some chick that knew the family, and she was always around. We hooked up every now and then, but lately she's been calling nonstop. She, like my father, knew way too much about Korrine when neither of them should know shit unless they were watching me." Tony stood from his recliner and started to pace.

Jake watched Tony pace. "You think your father and Misty have been communicating. But what would be their reason for wanting you away from Korrine?" Jake stated with a look of confusion written all over his face.

They both thought for a few seconds before they both answered in unison, "Money."

"Misty needs it," Tony added.

"And your father has it."

"But what can either of them gain by me not being with Korrine?"

"We both know Misty Austin would do anything to stay in the life in which she has grown up accustomed, and she needs a husband. Her bed-hopping ways aren't going to last much longer. She isn't a spring chicken after all," Jake stated with a smirk.

"Right, that's reason enough for Misty to want Korrine out of the way, so she can try to get her hooks into my wallet, but why would my father care?" Tony said growing tired of all the unanswered questions.

Jake shrugged his shoulders, "other than him being a bigot?" Jake responded matter-of-factly.

"It couldn't be just that, Jake. As much as I dislike the bastard, he's smart. He wouldn't come to me like he did just because Korrine is black. No, this has something to do with business. He kept bringing it up, even more than usual. He had a sense of urgency like I've never seen in him." Tony shook his head, his brown eyes becoming clouded as the pieces of the puzzle just wouldn't shift into place.

"He wants me to give over my shares, but why now? He has never mentioned my shares before. He only wanted me to take over the company, but I thought he would let it go once I made my first million on my own. He hasn't brought the business up in years, and never has he mentioned my shares. We all have shares." Jake nodded in agreement as Tony continued. "Now all of a sudden he's here telling me that I need to be married and talking about my shares...why?"

Tony was clearly frustrated. His face was stricken with worry lines, and his eyes had dark rings under them. His hair was all messy from him constantly running his hands through it in exasperation. There was still so many unanswered questions.

"Why, indeed, is the question...I need to get access to Cameron Corps financials. If this is about money, then that's where we need to look," Jake stated then paused. "What about

Korrine's stalker? Do you think that your father had something to do with that too?"

"The stalker did come from nowhere...and Korrine doesn't have an enemy in the world...except for maybe Misty...." Tony looked at Jake.

"Could Misty be behind this stalking thing?" Jake asked.

"Why would she stalk Korrine? It doesn't make any sense. But she was acting super disturbed the last time I saw her. She was almost desperate...ranting like a lunatic in my office."

"What all did she say?"

"Come to think of it, she knew way too much about Korrine. She knew she was a designer and everything. Those are things she shouldn't have known because I hadn't seen Misty in weeks...maybe even months...before I started dating Korrine."

"These are things you should've told me, buddy," Jake said going back to his computer screen.

"I thought it was Steve," Tony replied deprecatingly.

"Jealousy can do that to a man."

Tony quirked an eyebrow and stopped pacing. He looked over at his cousin, who was smirking as he typed furiously on his keyboard. "What is this about me being jealous? I'm not jealous of that asshole. He can't take my girl."

Jake smirked even harder and looked at Tony. "Buddy, it isn't about if he can take your girl; it's about the fact that he has the audacity to try. Korrine is a beautiful woman, men are going to give her attention, and you are not going to like it."

"Of course I'm not going to like it! What sane man wants his woman being ogled by other men? Like when that asshole Jeff was grinding all over her," Tony said with fury in his voice. "I wanted to bash his head in but I didn't. And that motherfucker deserved more after the things he said about her. His ass better be glad he's not in a coma somewhere."

"Wait, Jeff….Jeff who?" Jake asked sitting up.

"Jeffery Langston…smug asshole. But no worries, I put that dick in his place. I haven't seen or heard from him since," Tony replied.

"First, you should've told me about that too. We know Jeff is a vindictive little shit. He could've easily contacted your father."

"Why would he want to? Korrine and I weren't even dating at that point," Tony responded brushing Jake's comment away.

"Did you threaten him?"

"Wouldn't you?"

"You can't beat down and threaten every man that 'ogles' Korrine. Again, she is a beautiful woman, and that is something that *will* happen. Believe me, buddy, you're going to have to learn to relax because you can't control every aspect of life," Jake sighed. "Look, I'm going to look into Jeff. Like I said, he can be a vindictive piece of work. So you threatening him may not have gone away as easily as you thought."

Tony looked at his cousin. He knew he was right, but he just didn't want to admit that to the smirking bastard. He wasn't trying to control Korrine. He only wanted to control himself and the intense feelings and emotions he had when he was around her. Tony suddenly felt exhausted. Could he have brought all this trouble to sweet Korrine? She said herself that she didn't have anyone in her life that would stalk her in her past or present. It was he who had all the bimbos, silver spoon jerk offs, and a crazy father lurking.

Shit, maybe this is my fault.

He had to make things right with Korrine before any of these people hurt her.

CHAPTER 18

Misty

"I have had enough of this bullshit!" Misty was still steaming mad long after hanging up with Anderson Cameron. Her father's dirty dealings had gotten her into another mess. This time it wasn't as simple as a quick lay with some police chief or high up politician to get him out of the mess. He spent all of his time and the family's money being irresponsible. He was supposed to be the head of the family, but instead he was the deadbeat that brought shame on the family name whenever he had the chance. Misty didn't consider herself the bimbo or the good time girl that she was known for. She's had to clean up her father's messes since she turned seventeen. Unfortunately, she used her body instead of her brain to get those messes cleaned up, so now she was stuck looking after a man that should've been protecting her. Now he was knee deep in some investment scheme with Anderson Cameron, and they needed Tony's shares to pull off a cover-up. Tony didn't know that most of his father's shares were sold; he had to cover-up his debt and horrible investment deals. In order to regain controlling shares of the company, he needed Tony's.

He knew that Tony wouldn't just hand them over no questions asked like his wife did. No, he would want an explanation, and Anderson wouldn't give him that. So, he needed someone close to Tony that had access to his private information. A wife, girlfriend...hell, Anderson would take baby mama at this point...someone Anderson could control and get the information from. Problem was, Tony didn't have a wife or girlfriend that Anderson could control. But if Misty Austin would've done her damn job dragging him to the altar, or, at the very least, being a constant companion, his problem and her father's problem would've been solved. But that damn designer was messing up his head and getting in the way. Misty hoped that Korrine was just a passing phase, a conquest like all the others, but she had lasted months...way longer than any other.

Now with a hope of a relationship going down the drain, Misty thought the old fake pregnancy would get him to fall in line. But she couldn't get the bastard back in bed with her because of that black bitch! Misty was okay with Tony's flings, as long as he came back to her. She didn't mean to fall for him, but that is exactly what she did. She put up with a lot to keep Tony in her life, and now it was all for nothing.

Korrine Taylor had to go; she needed to be out of the way. Misty picked up the phone and dialed the man that needed to get the job done.

"I need this done ASAP. You told me she wouldn't be interested in Tony because she was a long term type. You said that she wouldn't want some playboy with women all over the place, you said-"

Misty was interrupted. "She is the relationship type, but apparently so is he...now. Let's not forget that *you* said he was a love them and leave them type, that he didn't keep a woman around for more than a month. I can't even get close to her. Every time I turn around, I'm looking at Antonio Fuckin' Cameron. He's always around!" Steve's face was beet red as he screamed at Misty.

"I don't give a damn, Steve!" Misty yelled into the phone. "You said that you could get her out of the way; that you were just her type; that she wouldn't fall for a guy like him with you around. It's been four months, and they are as close as ever."

"Look, you're the one who said that if she had problems he wouldn't want to be bothered. I set up all the stupid notes and phone calls. But instead of her leaving him, she ran straight into his arms. The stalking was *your* idea. He just became more protective. You pushed him right to her!" Steve yelled back.

"The stalking would've worked if the letters would've been more threatening. She was hardly afraid," Misty seethed throwing her hands in the air.

"Of course she was afraid; she's still afraid. They both are. Tony has a team of guys watching her. I can't even get close to her to plant any more letters without anyone seeing me and being suspicious. This is becoming too much. I just wanted Korrine for myself. I can't be caught up in whatever else you have going on. Korrine was supposed to turn to me as a friend so we could get close in her time of need. That didn't happen; now she has bodyguards. I'm a business man. I can't be mixed up in this crazy scheme of yours anymore, Misty."

"Did you forget the information that I have on you Steve? Now with your involvement in this, I can ruin you completely." Misty sneered narrowing her eyes.

"You can't turn me in without implicating yourself, and we both know you're smarter than that. So what if my good-for-nothing-wife ran off with my brother and they almost destroyed my business with their investment schemes. Worse things have happened. I've lived in shame for too long to get mixed up in this because of a threat to my business was dumb of me. I should've never gotten involved with the likes of you. I'm done." Steve hung up the phone.

Misty slammed her hand into the wall as if she was slapping Steve's face. She threw her phone across the room and screamed at the top of her lungs. "ARRRGHH!"

She couldn't believe that she had been hung up on for the second time tonight. The information she had on the investment scheme, plus what she planted to make it look like Steve hurt his wife, should've been enough to keep him in line.

Blackmail just didn't work like it used to.

She would have to get her hands dirty on this one. Since the stalking wasn't working, she needed to get Korrine out of the way on a more permanent basis.

****

Jake had searched through almost all of Cameron Corps documents, and they were perfect…too perfect. Someone was doctoring the financials, and he had a good idea who, but why? Jake informed Tony what he found and decided to crash for the night. He stayed in Tony's guest room, not wanting to drive. Tony was still awake. Although he was exhausted, he couldn't sleep. The thought of him being the reason Korrine was being stalked was making him physically ill. He needed to talk to Korrine and tell her everything.

"Hello?" Korrine answered in a sleep ridden voice.

"Hey, sweetness, it's me. Sorry to wake you, but I really need to talk."

"It's late, Tony. Can't we do this tomorrow? It's...1 am."

"I know, baby, but it's really important. It can't wait until tomorrow. You really need to know what's been going on," Tony said sounding almost desperate, pacing back and forth in his apartment.

"Okay," Korrine yawned. "What's going on, Tony?"

"Jake and I have been doing some digging, and we think we may know who is behind your stalking."

"Steve?" Korrine asked feeling more awake.

"No, I don't think it is Steve...Why do you all of a sudden think it's Steve?" Tony asked stopping his pacing.

Korrine finally told Tony about the intense conversation she and Steve had before he walked in the last time she saw Steve. She let him know how suspicious Steve had been acting lately, how the calls only come when he's not around, and how the notes were always left when he had been around.

After everything Korrine told him, he had to reconsider that maybe Steve was involved somehow. He really had too much information going around his head at the moment. He wasn't thinking clearly.

"Tony, are you still there?" Korrine asked.

"Yea, baby, I'm here. Korrine, I really need to see you; there is so much going on, and I know it's late, baby, and you're mad, but I need to see you."

"Oh-kay...I'll be here...Tony?"

"Yea, sweetness?"

"Be safe, okay? See you soon."

CHAPTER 19

Korrine

Once Korrine hung up the phone, she decided to get up and make some coffee. If she and Tony were going to have this much needed talk, she better be wide awake, and that meant coffee was a must.

Korrine went to her kitchen, popped a k-cup in her coffee maker, and headed back to her bathroom to freshen up. Just as she was finishing up in the bathroom, she decided that maybe coffee wasn't strong enough for the conversation she was about to have. So she decided to look for the stash of liquor she knew Brandon and Lauren always had when they came over.

"Hmm...now if I was a bottle of liquor, where would I be?" Korrine said out loud.

It had been ten minutes after she drank her coffee, and she still couldn't find the bottle of cherry flavored vodka that she knew Brandon left the last time he was over.

Maybe I should just call and ask Brandon. He's probably still awake. Korrine giggled at her thoughts. *Nah, if he is awake, he's probably doing something naughty.*

She missed Brandon. He had been spending a lot of Q-T time with his new beau and Korrine, knowing what the honeymoon stage of a new relationship could be like, didn't want to interfere. Even though her honeymoon didn't last, she didn't want to shatter anyone else's illusion of love. Come to think of it, Korrine hadn't seen much of Brandon or Lauren. She had been so wrapped up in Tony that she was neglecting her friendships. Although talking to Lauren while she was fighting with her cousin was a bit awkward at first, Lauren was a good friend and tried to see both sides of the argument without giving Korrine a hard time. She really did have good friends.

A knock on the door brought Korrine out of her thoughts and back to the present. She looked at her clock, thinking, *Damn, Tony got here fast. If we make up, I need to talk to him about his speeding.* Korrine smiled at the thought of them making up. Her heart thumped in her chest. She wanted to see

Tony. Not seeing him every day or talking to him was a new kind of torture, and she just didn't think she had the strength to endure it any longer. Although she was still upset about him calling her ungrateful, she could put her big girl panties on and talk to him instead of storming off and not speaking to him. He was just so damn stubborn, and so was she. Two stubborn people were bound to bump heads. But if this was going to work, they would have to learn to compromise with each other. They were both passionate people that loved hard and with everything they had in them. So, it made sense that feelings that explosive could be more than intense. Korrine hoped they could work out their differences; she really missed Tony these past couple of days.

Korrine smiled wide as she swung open the door.

Korrine's smile quickly fell from her face when she opened the door and saw a strange woman standing there.

"May I help you?" Korrine asked closing the door to just a crack.

"Why, yes, you absolutely can," the woman replied with an evil grin spreading across her face.

Korrine didn't like the look on the woman's face or in her eyes. She didn't recognize the leggy blond with the too tight dress. But the woman seemed to be familiar with her, and Korrine didn't like that feeling at all.

She moved to shut the door all the way when the woman caught Korrine off guard and shoved the door, knocking Korrine off balance while quickly moving inside.

The woman pulled a gun as her evil smile grew wider. Gasping, Korrine took a step back shaking her head at the woman. "Who-who are you?! What do you want?!" Korrine asked growing frantic.

The woman let out a maniacal laugh that showed she was clearly disturbed before dropping her handbag on the floor while wiping at the invisible lint on her short bandage dress.

"Oh, we aren't so tough, are we 'sweetness'? I overestimated you. Since you are from South Dallas, I just knew I would have to 'scrap' a little."

Korrine narrowed her eyes at the woman's blatant bigotry. "I don't know what you want, but you can take it and leave," she hissed through bated breath.

"Oh, I'm going to do just that and more, Korrine. I'm Misty, by the way. We haven't been introduced since Tony has been hiding you away. You see, I've been seeing Tony for quite some time, and I was planning on marrying him. We have a lot in common, he and I. Our families go way back, but he seems to have gotten distracted and strayed from my plans of matrimony. I tried to get him to see that you weren't on his level. A man of his caliber needs someone with a name and standing in the community. Tony needs me, and I need him. You don't have the pedigree that I have." Misty said this as if it was the sanest explanation in the world.

Korrine looked at the woman with a wide-eyed expression. Misty was rambling on as if she should know what the hell she was going on about.

"Misty, is it?" Korrine asked hesitantly. "Look, Tony and I aren't even dating anymore. We weren't even anything official. So I really don't know why you are in my house holding me at gunpoint. None of this makes any sense to me."

Korrine, with her hands in the air, backed away, stumbling over an end table by the door and knocking over a lamp. The sound of the lamp crashing to the floor made both women jump. Misty's hand shook slightly, giving away her true demeanor. She may have seemed calm, but the look in her eyes was pure insanity.

Korrine knew she had to stall this crazy person. Tony was on his way and would be there any moment. All she had to do was keep this heffa talking, and then she would be free from this deranged individual.

"I really don't know what's going on or why you are here. Tony never mentioned he was getting married or even thinking about marriage. That's not something we talked about."

Misty gave another high-pitched laugh. "You aren't really that smart, are you? I don't have time to explain anything to you right now. So *you* look, Tony is probably on his way. I know the goons he has watching this place will be back from their shift change at any moment, so we need to get out of here."

Goons? Tony has someone watching my place? Why didn't he tell me? Obviously the threat was more serious than I thought, since this crazy bitch is here with a gun. How does she know Tony is on his way? Korrine's thoughts were all over the place. The questions were popping in her head so fast that she didn't realize that Misty was about to slap her.

Whack!

Misty's hand came hard across Korrine's face, making her stumble back once again. "I said let's move, bitch! Don't just stand there daydreaming! I don't have time for this shit!"

Korrine stumbled back but didn't fall. She caught herself, seething with anger. *This bitch thinks she's bad with a gun. But if it's the last thing I do, I'm going to knock her the fuck out!* Korrine gathered her composure and narrowed her eyes at Misty before slowly moving toward the door. Once at the door, Korrine whirled around trying to catch Misty off guard, pushing her with all the strength she could muster. But Misty was watching closely and saw the move coming. Misty side stepped her and, although Korrine was able to knock her slightly off balance, Misty didn't lose her grip on the gun.

She smirked at Korrine and pushed her in the back. "Tsk tsk, 'sweetness.' That wasn't so sweet. You better be glad I still need to get you out of here, or I would put a bullet in your pretty little head. Now move, and don't try anything else or, so help me, I will find another way to get *your body* out of this shithole you call an apartment."

As Misty led Korrine out the door into the stairwell, Korrine was trembling with fear, wondering how in the hell did she get into this mess, and how in the hell was she going to get out of it. Korrine was looking around trying to see if she had a way out, but there was no possible way she could get away from this maniac without being shot. Korrine knew once she was in a different location, it would lessen the probability of her surviving. She watched Law and Order, so she knew the deal. But she just couldn't think and she had no idea what to do. She never thought of herself as a weak woman, but as they made it out of the building through a side door, a tear of despair slipped down her cheek.

There was a car waiting right by the side entrance. Korrine lost hope. She was going to be kidnapped.

Misty pushed Korrine into the back seat, and slid in beside her. Korrine didn't see the face of the person driving the car before she felt an excruciating pain in her head and everything went black.

****

Korrine woke with a start. Her head was pounding and the room was dark. She couldn't move her arms or her legs; her whole body felt stiff. *Where the hell am I?*

Korrine moaned. She couldn't open her mouth all the way. *What the hell? Am I gagged?* Korrine started thrashing violently, but quickly stopped when the pounding in her head made her almost pass out. She tried moving her hands and legs, but she couldn't. She was tied to a chair. Korrine started to panic. She didn't know where she was and what was going on, and the throbbing in her head made tears fall down her cheeks. She was alone in what seemed like a warehouse of some kind. *Why was this happening?* Korrine tried to calm her breathing, but she couldn't manage to relax. The longer she sat there, the more frantic she became. Her breathing started to become erratic, the blackness started to creep in, and she passed out again.

CHAPTER 20

Misty

Misty was waiting in the penthouse suite of the fancy hotel, putting the rest of her plan in motion. She was done trying to save her stupid father and his no good associate.

They could all kiss her ass. She was going to hold Korrine for ransom and get on the first thing smokin'. There was no way in hell Tony was going to marry her or get her pregnant. That was wishful thinking and stupid on her part. However, she was done living in la-la land. She knew that Tony was in love with this girl when she followed them. Steve was stupid to think that he could ever pull any sane woman away from Antonio Cameron. If she had been thinking with her head and not her heart, she would have gotten as far away from this mess as she could. Now, that was exactly what she was going to do.

First things first, she made sure her alibi was tight for the disappearance of Korrine. Jeff Langston was an old friend of the family, and he hated Tony as much as she hated Korrine. He was all too happy to be her "get away" driver. He couldn't wait to get back at Tony by knocking the stuck up little bitch that he dealt with down a peg or two. Misty had just as much dirt on Jeff anyway. He had a penchant for young girls, especially a young under-aged Misty. She had pictures, text messages, and emails proving they had a relationship way before she was of age. It would ruin his family, but she didn't even have to blackmail him. All she had to do was cozy up to him, get him a drink or two, and tell him the plan. She should've just used him from the beginning, but he was a loose cannon who likes to brag about his revenge. So she had to still keep a close eye on him. Plus Steve had disappeared since their last heated conversation, so she had to make sure he was still under whatever rock he had himself under for a couple more days until she could get the hell out of Texas to somewhere tropical with no extradition laws.

"Hey, is the package still in the holding position?" Misty asked Jeff using a burner phone and code. She had dealt with many a corrupt politician and not so reputable men saving her father, and she knew exactly what to do in order to get the ransom drop. It was sad, really, but a skill nonetheless.

"I'm still holding. The package is in the location specified," Jeff replied. At least he was smart enough to speak in code like she told him to. He must really hate Tony to be following her instructions without any argument.

"Great, you have the other burner and the PC with the program. Use those and send the ransom message. Make sure you give him ten hours and wait the entire ten hours. Otherwise they may get suspicious. They should know the little bitch is missing now, so we need to make them sweat a little. So we just wait, make the call, give the instructions, and lay low until we can get the hell out of dodge."

"Right, I'll make the call, and I will text you when I get a response."

"Good, make sure that black bitch is uncomfortable, and I will wait for your text," Misty said hanging up.

This is going to be easier than I thought it would. Who knew Jeff could be so easily controlled? Maybe they could leave together...Nah, then she wouldn't have anyone to pin all this shit on. Oh well. Jeff would just have to be sacrificed for the greater good.

Misty was so wrapped up in her thoughts that she almost missed her phone ringing.

"Hello..."

"Misty, where the hell are you? Have you spoken to Tony? Apparently, Tony's little whore has disappeared. One of my people from the law enforcement there told me about it. What the hell is going on!?" Anderson all but yelled in the phone.

"I told you, *Anderson*, I haven't spoken to your son, and he refuses to take my calls. So why would I keep calling him?" Misty responded playing it cool.

"First of all, don't you ever talk to me in that manner. I will not be disrespected by trash like you. Now answer my fucking questions. Do you know what's going on?"

"I have no idea what you're talking about; I told you when we spoke last that your little plan wasn't working. My father and you will have to get yourselves out of this mess. I can't be involved anymore. My guy got spooked and called the whole thing off. So, I took his lead and decided it would probably be best if I did the same. But, you wouldn't know any of that because you hung up in my face and you, like your son, also refused my calls." Misty was goading Anderson into losing his composure. If she could get him talking, maybe she could pin something on him too.

"Listen, you little bitch!! We had a deal. You are going to help me get my son's shares, and you are going to do it quickly! Or I will do my best to ruin your entire life, and let's not forget about your family's name. You don't have a pot to piss in, and I will make sure everyone from Georgia to Texas knows all your dirty little secrets," Anderson yelled, seething.

Gotcha asshole, Misty thought with a smirk. Her plan was working; she made him believe that she had nothing to do with Korrine's unfortunate disappearance, got him talking and made him believe that she was no longer helping with his idiotic plan.

"I don't care who you tell or what you tell them. I. AM. DONE! Tell my father to clean up his own mess." Misty hung up in Anderson's face.

CHAPTER 21

Tony

Tony was speeding trying to get to Korrine's house; he missed his sweetness, even though it had only been a couple of days. He was tired of fighting his feelings for her; hell, he was tired of fighting with her. He needed to be lost in his woman, letting her know that she was his. Then they could deal with this shitstorm coming down on them together. Yeah, it may have been partly his fault that she was being stalked, but he would protect her with his life if he had to. Nothing was going to come between them again. That he was sure of.

Some of Jake's guys were running out of Korrine's apartment, frantically looking around. Tony became anxious when he saw the expressions on the faces of these well-trained men.

When Tony got to Korrine's, he knew something wasn't right. "What the hell is going on?" he said to no one in particular.

He knew that whatever was said to him was not going to be good news. His heart began to pound even harder and, when he saw Jake running up the stairs, his heart that was beating so frantically instantly dropped to his stomach.

"Jake?! Where's Korri?!" Tony was rambling with fear growing inside of him at a rapid pace. "Why are you here? I just left you at the house!"

"Buddy, Korri is gone-"

"WHAT?!" he shouted. "How do you know she didn't just leave?!"

"Somebody got to her. They knew about my guys, Tony," Jake stated trying to remain calm for his cousin.

"Seems one of her neighbors saw Korrine being pushed down the back stairwell by a woman that she didn't recognize. The lady also said she thinks she may have seen a gun but can't be sure."

"Why can't she be sure?" Tony asked.

"She's an older lady, probably early seventies. Her eyes aren't what they used to be, but she knows Korri. She said Korri didn't even realize she was there, and neither did the other lady."

"Did the lady get a good look at who Korri was with?"

"Yep, blond with a tight dress."

"Fuckin' hell!!" Tony yelled.

"I thought the same thing…Misty," Jake replied.

"Why is she doing this? She had to have a gun, Jake. There is no way in hell Korri would have gone with her just willingly. Damn it!" Tony roared with frustration.

"It's okay, cousin. We will find her. I promise you that!" Jake assured him.

****

Jake

It hadn't been but a few hours since Korrine had been forced out of her apartment. Jake and his guys were looking at the security footage in Korri's building, but Misty was smarter than she looked. The cameras had been disabled at the time she led Korrine out of the building. She had to have had help. There was no way she was smart enough to know how to work a security system. Although the system wasn't that high tech, you would still have to know how to hack into the system. Who in the hell was helping this silly bitch? Both Tony and Jake were beyond frustrated with the lack of information they were finding. Misty had done one hell of a job covering her tracks. She also must have been watching Korrine and Tony for some time in order to pull off taking her right under Jake's guys' noses. They were professionals who never should've been caught off guard the way they were. It was unacceptable, and Jake was livid. They knew that Korrine was a high priority. Even though she hadn't had any direct contact with her stalker, they were still supposed to keep a watch on her apartment and studio. They had to wait for this psycho to slip up in the act; instead, they slipped right in under their nose and took her. Misty had to have been watching her apartment to know the exact moment to slip in unnoticed. Korrine was a creature of habit, after all; she rarely did anything but work and go home, so that's what made it easy to keep an eye on her. Unfortunately, it also made it easy to stalk her. Jake constantly told her to switch up her routine, but she was one of the most stubborn people he had ever met. He and Tony agreed that she didn't take her stalking as seriously as she should have, and now they were stuck going over three months' worth of information from the PI, as well as taps and security cameras around Korri's studio and apartment. They knew the person responsible was Misty. But who in the hell could she be working with, and where the hell was she? Nobody could pinpoint her location, and that was more than worrying to both Tony and Jake.

"Tell me what you got," Jake stated into the phone.

"A lot, boss. First, your uncle has been a very busy man; he and Misty have been in contact for the past eight months. I also looked into the financials of Cameron Corp, and you were right," Mike, Jake's head of IT, stated. "Whoever cooked the books did a bang up job, but I found the discrepancies. It seems like Tony is actually the majority owner of shares in the company. His dad, although very discreetly, has sold his shares little by little, and he even sold Mrs. Cameron's shares as well."

"Shit, this is way more complicated than I thought," Jake sighed. "How long has my dear uncle been selling off his company shares?"

"A little over a year," Mike replied.

"Did you find any connection to Misty?" Jake asked.

"Yep, I was just getting to that. Seems like Mr. Cameron started selling his shares after making a major bad investment. He did fly under the radar with the investment, which is why nobody really knows about it, except Mr. Gregory Austin. He was on the board of directors for the investment that was supposed to garner millions. But to me it looks to be some elaborate pyramid scheme. They were getting money from Peter to pay Paul...just on a larger scale. The investment was supposed to be for some building complex in Florida. The scheme seemed to be going just fine until Austin got greedy and got involved with some unsavory characters. He got in over his head, and now he and your uncle owe some very bad people a lot of money."

"So who was he selling off the shares to?" Jake asked.

"He was selling them off in bits and pieces, but not to any one individual or company. So nobody could actually take over Cameron Corp, but he just doesn't have controlling shares anymore; Tony does. With the shares your grandfather left him, and those his mother also gave him out of hers, he now has the majority of the shares…even more than your father and uncle," Mike stated.

"So let me get this straight…Tony has controlling shares of the family corporation and his dad is trying to get those shares by using Misty?"

"Yeah, in so many words. However, Misty seems to have gone rogue. Since we knew she took Korrine, we tapped her phone. Misty received one phone call from your uncle. She's pretending not to know anything about Korrine's disappearance; she also said that she was done with him and her father. She's downtown in the penthouse suite. She doesn't know we're on to her yet, so we have an advantage."

"Thanks, Mike. You have connected a lot of dots for me. I appreciate it greatly. You know how I feel about family, and Korrine is family," Jake said.

"No thanks needed, boss. That's what you pay me for. The guys are sitting on Misty's location, but we haven't seen any sign of Korri and Misty hasn't made a move yet. What do you want us to do?"

"Sit tight. Make sure the guys don't let her get the slip on them this time, or there will be hell to pay."

"Got it, boss!"

CHAPTER 22

Tony

Tony disconnected the call from Jake; it would seem his father had been a very busy man indeed. However, although Misty didn't seem to be working with him any longer, she damn sure is the one who took Korrine. Now they needed to figure out the motive behind his father's involvement, but they couldn't figure out why Misty was still involved if she cut ties with the dirty bastard. Jake's guys were sitting on Misty, and she hadn't made a move or used her phone all day. If those asses let her get away this time, they would definitely have hell to pay. She was the only lead they had to finding Korri, especially since nobody had seen or heard from Steve. His assistant claimed he left for Houston two days before and she hadn't heard from him since. None of Jake or Tony's contacts in Houston had located him. It seems old Stevie boy gave them the slip. If he had any idea what Misty was up to, he left before the plan was set in motion.

It was time to pay Misty a little visit. Just before Tony was about to leave, he got a phone call.

"Hello?"

"Hello…" Tony immediately realized that the caller was speaking into a voice changer, so he just waited, held his breath in anxiety and listened. "I think I have something that belongs to you. I need you to cooperate and this can end quickly and quietly without anyone getting hurt. Don't call the authorities or your nosey ass cousin, or the only thing you will need to worry about is finding her body."

"What do you want?"

"Money… one million to be exact. I will contact you on the phone left at the front desk of your building with instructions of the drop off location and the time." The caller disconnected before Tony had a chance to ask any more questions.

"Damn it!" Tony yelled as he slammed his phone down, rushing to the front desk of his building. He knew he wouldn't have to tell Jake about the call. They knew this was about money, and that it was only a matter of time before that is exactly what they asked for, so they had been waiting for it. Jake put a trace on Tony's phone just to prepare for this situation.

Tony reached the front desk of his building and was handed the phone without asking. The guy behind the counter just nodded in the direction of one of Jake's guys, indicating he knew what was going on. As soon as Tony retrieved the phone, it began ringing. It was a burner phone so they wouldn't be able to trace the call, but at least the surveillance on his building should give them a clue as to who dropped the phone off.

Before Tony could say hello, the caller gave him directions on where the next phone pickup would be. The caller let him know that he had ten hours to retrieve the money. At the end of the ten hours, he would receive another call. Tony didn't have time to explain that he couldn't get that amount of money in such a short period of time. But he knew Korrine's life depended on him coming through with the money, so he would do what he had to do to make sure he had the cash. Tony was going to have to call in a lot of favors to make sure he had the unmarked bills. He knew that it was a possibility that he may not be able to recover the money if the plan backfired, but he didn't care about the money. Tony had to get his woman back!

****

It was good that Tony knew the right people. Working with professional athletes, being a semi-celebrity and a very rich man in his own right got him acquainted with quite a few people that could be discreet and help him get exactly what he needed. In a couple of hours, Tony would have everything he needed to make the drop. Then all he would have to do was wait for the phone call that would tell him when and where to leave the money.

Tony wasn't a fool; he knew for certain that Misty was behind this whole thing, but he didn't know who was helping her. Jake's guys had been sitting on Misty since they found her location in the downtown hotel suite a few hours ago. She hadn't made so much as an attempt to leave the building; she ordered room service and she never used her cell phone. Jake pulled some strings with an old buddy from the service and got a rushed APB put out on Steve in connection to Korrine's stalking case. He had been found in south Texas trying to make his way across the border. He had no idea Korrine was missing, but with the evidence Jake's guys had managed to dig up on him, Steve was more than happy to cooperate so he wouldn't be indicted for the kidnapping. With everything going on and the knowledge that Steve was no longer helping Misty, Tony had no idea who had Korrine and he was still waiting for the drop information from the mysterious caller.

Tony didn't think his father would sink so low as to kidnap someone. No, the Cameron name meant too much to him, so he wouldn't do anything so bold as to jeopardize the name. He just couldn't wrap his head around who would be so desperate to help Misty to do this.

CHAPTER 23

Korrine

Korrine had no idea who would do this. After waking with a start, her hands and feet were still tied to a chair and her head was full on banging. Her vision was blurred a little, and she still didn't recognize where she was.

She heard footsteps coming and began to shake in fear. Korrine had no idea what was coming her way or who.

"Hey there, sunshine. Are you awake yet?" Jeff asked taking the gag out of Korrine's mouth. His face was covered, so Korrine wouldn't be able to recognize him; they hadn't spent enough time together to be able to identify his voice.

Korrine opened her eyes slowly afraid of what she might see, but it was a man in a mask. It wasn't the blond from before, and it wasn't Steve. Steve was shorter and thinner than the man standing before her. Korrine had no idea who this person was.

"Who are you?" Korrine asked slowly. "And what do you want with me?"

"Now, now. I'm not one of those stupid criminals that tell all their plans to the hostage just so you know what's going on. No, I like to keep them guessing; makes the experience more fun," Jeff said with a sinister laugh.

"Look, I don't have any family," Korrine stammered, as the throbbing pain in her head was nearing unbearable. "I'm sure I don't have the kind of money that warrants a hostage situation. So I really don't have a clue as to what you think you can get from holding me here."

"Like I said, you don't need to know any plans," Jeff hissed, placing the gag back in Korrine's mouth. She didn't struggle, but worry raced through her body as he continued. "But please believe you are worth holding hostage. Now, I think that's enough conversation for now. It's time for you to shut up so I can get this shit done."

Korrine knew something wasn't right because she could feel her head spinning. She didn't know how long it had been since she was taken, but she knew she needed medical attention because it was hard for her to remain conscious and her vision was still blurry. Just when her vision started to focus more, she heard the man cursing.

"Fuck! Where is this bitch? Nobody is answering the phones!"

Jeff paced back and forth, trying to figure out what he missed. At exactly ten hours, he called the phone number

Misty gave him that was supposed to be Tony's burner phone. But there was no answer. Maybe Tony didn't love Korrine as much as Misty claimed. Why wouldn't he answer a ransom call? Jeff called the phone several times before calling the burner phone Misty had.

"Fuck!" he cursed as there was no answer there either. Jeff had no idea what was going on, but he had a bad feeling about this whole situation.

Korrine started to cry, letting the tears silently slip down her face as she came to realize her captor was slowly losing his mind. He was pacing and cursing and making calls, but he never talked to anyone. She was terrified that whatever this lunatic had planned was falling apart, and she was about to be a casualty. She was tied to the chair so tight that her hands and feet were numb, and she definitely couldn't reason with a crazy person. Korrine had come to the very real conclusion that she just may die here today. She sent up a prayer to God, asking if she had been a good enough person to make it to heaven, if she could be reunited with her mother and father, and that Brandon and Lauren would forgive her for leaving them and lean on each other for support. And her last prayer was for Tony, that this incredibly strong man would remain strong and someday find someone worthy of his love and over protectiveness.

Thinking about her love for Brandon, Lauryn, and Tony, Korrine smiled to herself as the tears flowed freely.

"What the hell are you smiling about?!" Jeff all but snarled at Korrine.

Korrine couldn't answer him because she had a gag in her mouth, so she remained silent. She didn't want to agitate the crazy man more than he already was.

Jeff snatched the gag out of Korrine's mouth.

"This is your fault. If Tony loved you, he would have paid the damn ransom! Now, what the fuck am I going to do?! I'm stuck here with you! I have got to find a way out of this mess!"

He was ranting and raving and acting like the lunatic he was. Korrine whimpered as she tried not to have a full on breakdown.

"I have to get out of here," Jeff huffed. He put the gag back in Korrine's mouth and he started throwing things in a duffel bag when the burner phone started to ring. "Yes?!" Jeff shouted into the phone.

There was silence on the other end, and Jeff started to panic. He dropped the phone and started hastily grabbing anything that would incriminate him. He picked up the duffel bag and headed towards the door.

"Sorry, but you're not worth all this trouble," Jeff stated as he headed towards the door, leaving a sobbing Korrine tied to the chair in the abandoned warehouse.

****

Misty

Misty looked in the mirror at her new brown bob haircut. She would miss her long blond tresses that made her look like a real life Barbie. *Yeah, well, that didn't get me what I needed. So maybe this look will suit me better,* Misty thought to herself as she placed brown contacts over her blue eyes. She dressed in a baggy jumpsuit and ballet flats. The real Misty wouldn't be caught dead in this outfit, but it made her unrecognizable. She couldn't wear her signature tight bandage dress, or someone would definitely know it was her.

Misty got the burner phone to place the ransom call. She had given Jeff a bogus number, knowing the burner phone would only be used once and then replaced with another. He was so caught up in her manipulations that he couldn't see straight. Jeff would never see the double-cross coming until it was too late. The burner phone, having Jeff stay with Korrine in the abandoned building, having him call in the first ransom…it was all part of the set-up. Who in the hell asked for money in a bag when money in an account was much more accessible? Why risk someone seeing you or putting a tracker in the bag? Jeff was so gullible. Misty had it all worked out; knowing some not so good people came in handy from time to time. You paid a fee, and they did the job with no questions asked. She paid a pretty penny for the security feed to Korrine's apartment to be cut, and she paid a hefty price for a new identity, along with a passport, credit cards, and an account in the same name.

Misty left the hotel. She knew they would be waiting for her, but Misty Austin would never leave the hotel because her new identity, Victoria McCoy, was already on the other side of town in an abandoned warehouse district making a ransom call.

Misty made her way to the airport parking in a long-term garage. As she maneuvered the car into a secluded spot, she made the call.

"Hello," Tony answered sounding almost desperate.

"Change of plans…I want you to wire the money to an account," Misty ordered using the voice scrambler.

"That wasn't the deal!" Tony yelled. "How do I know Korrine is even still alive?"

"I'm running this show, and the bitch *is* alive! But she won't be for long if I don't get my money!"

"How do I know you won't kill her as soon as you get your money if she's still alive? I'm not a stupid man. I need proof of life before you get a dime."

Misty knew that was coming. That's why she had a camera set up on Korrine, and it was also there to help Jeff take the fall since he was the only one there at the location.

"I'll send a live feed to you of your precious woman, and then I want my money," Misty replied rolling her eyes.

Misty disconnected and sent the feed to Tony of Korrine tied to a chair. Jeff wasn't in the frame, so it was helpful. Then she placed another call to Tony.

"You got what you asked for. Now give me my money," Misty sneered with narrowed eyes.

"But if I give you the money, how will I find Korrine?"

"I will give you the account number. As soon as the money is transferred, you will automatically get coordinates to where you can find the girl."

"Unharmed?" Tony confirmed.

"Unharmed. I have nothing to gain from hurting the girl. I just want my money." Misty said smirking.

Misty gave the account number to Tony and disconnected. As soon as she got the confirmation, she texted the location of the warehouse where Jeff had Korrine. Misty then made a call to Jeff. Once he answered the call, she dropped the burner in a trash can and made her way inside the airport.

CHAPTER 24

Tony

As soon as the location was sent, Tony sent Mike—Jake's IT guy—all of the information he received for the ransom. It was odd that the caller switched the way they wanted the money. Dropping the money would have been easier for them to pick up whoever had Korrine. But it looked as if the kidnapper—Misty—must've realized that and made the change. It didn't matter; Mike could still trace the money through the account Tony was given. He was absolutely positive that Misty couldn't be this smart and had to have help. But she would be caught…of that he was sure.

As the blacked out van pulled up to the location, Jake and his men were suiting up along with Tony, who refused to stay behind.

"All right guys, stay alert; we have no idea who is in the building besides Korrine," Jake sternly stated. "She hasn't been moved, and the feed is still live. But since there isn't any sound, we can't be sure what we're dealing with."

The guys were all business; they all felt responsible for letting Korrine get kidnapped on their watch. They knew this was their only shot to get Korrine out, and they weren't taking any more chances with her safety.

"We have a layout of the building; it should be a straight shot once we get inside. There is a corridor leading to a spacious open room with another corridor leading to an office in the back. It is logical to think Korri is being held in the back office, since that is the only closed off room," Jake instructed his team. "There is another hallway leading to a back exit, so we will have three guys bring up the rear and cover that exit.

Remember to keep your eyes open and watch each other's back."

"No man left behind! Let's get it!" they all responded in unison.

The guys filed out of the two vans that were parked on the side of the building. There weren't any cars visible, and the area looked to be completely deserted. This place seemed too far out for even the homeless to inhabit. It was still and quiet, giving off an eerie silence. The men gave each other hand signals to move out. Three guys headed around to the back of the building while two others headed to a building across the street to the rooftop.

Tony, Jake, and his men headed quietly into the building under the watchful eye of Mike. Everyone had earpieces in so they could communicate. Mike let them know Korri was still tied up and she had stopped struggling.

Tony already had a sense of urgency; but with Mike informing them that Korri stopped fighting, he knew he had to get to his sweetness.

The men moved efficiently through the building, looking out for any threats. None were found. The building seemed to be completely vacant. Jake did a quick sweep heading toward the office in the back of the warehouse with Tony following close behind. When they reached the office, they found Korrine tied to the chair. She wasn't moving, but she was still breathing.

Tony rushed to her side, cutting the ropes from her wrists and legs while removing the gag from her mouth. He held her in his arms, praying that she would show him those beautiful hazel eyes.

"Baby, wake up. I'm here, sweetness...I'm so sorry I couldn't protect you, baby," Tony pleaded with Korrine as his eyes welled with tears. "I love you, Korrine...please don't give up on me...I need you...Baby, open your eyes,"

Korrine's eyes slowly opened, and a small smile graced her lips.

"Superman...I love you too." Korri's eyes slowly shut again, and she was enveloped into darkness.

Tony started to panic, seeing Korrine lose consciousness. Just as he picked Korrine up, Tony heard Jake's walkie go off.

"Jake, we've got movement on the exterior of the building. Someone is running towards the railroad tracks on the west side of the warehouse!"

"Somebody call this in! Follow and stop the perp before they reach those tracks. It's an active freight line, so he can hop the rails and be lost to us forever…move now!" Jake yelled.

"It's already done, boss. The locals are on their way. They should be here in less than five," Mike responded.

"I can't wait another five minutes, Jake. I have got to get Korri to a hospital. She has a deep gash in her head, and it's swollen. She needs medical attention quickly," Tony said moving towards the exit with Korrine in his arms.

Jake was moving behind Tony. "Get her to the hospital, buddy. I'll take care of things here, and be there as soon as I wrap things up with the locals."

****

Jake slowly approached the suspect that his guys apprehended and turned over to the local police officers. The whole area was roped off with yellow tape, and the FBI had been called in. Jake didn't mind all the police around now because his work was done. Korri was safe, and now they had to follow the money to find Misty. However, he needed to know who the second player was that helped Misty hold Korrine captive.

When Jake reached the suspect, he was not surprised in the least.

"Jeffery Langston, how in the hell did you get wrapped up in this shit?" Jake questioned but knowing the answer.

"Fuck you," Jeff stated simply. "I want a lawyer."

"Lawyer? You are so passed innocent until proven guilty it's laughable. Do you know how much shit you're in? We found you at the scene of a kidnapping with a burner phone with a call history connecting you to making a ransom demand. Not only that, but you also left the victim half dead. If she dies, you better hope prison is in your future because if you get off..." Jake let the threat die off. Besides, there were Feds around. If this cocksucker by a miracle got acquitted, Jake would make sure he disappeared off the face of this earth.

Jeff saw the look in Jake's eyes. He knew if he didn't play his cards right he would surely end up dead. He didn't have the support of his family anymore, which is why he had to go along with this stupid ass plan in the first place! By the way, where the hell was Misty?

"I want a deal...and I will tell everything I know."

"Deal...fuckin' pussy. You better hope you're behind bars when I tell Tony you were involved in this." Jake said disgustedly as he walked away.

"Hey! Get me a lawyer!" Jeff screamed hysterically. "I need a deal! Give me my deal!!"

****

Tony ran towards one of the vans and hopped in, stowing Korrine in the back and instructing Mike to drive to the nearest emergency room. He was whispering words of love and encouragement all the way to the hospital. It seemed like an eternity before they reached the ER, but Tony knew it wasn't longer than fifteen minutes. Mike drove like a bat out of hell to get there.

Once they pulled up in front of the hospital, Tony hopped out of the van with Korri cradled in his arms before the vehicle even came to a complete stop. He rushed in, screaming for a doctor. The nurses took Korrine from Tony and placed her on a gurney, rushing her behind double doors and out of his line of sight. Tony crumpled to the ground to his knees and prayed to God that he would get to hold his sweetness again, and to look in her eyes and tell her he loved her.

Before he knew it, tears were flowing down his face and he felt himself shaking. Tony took a deep breath to gain his composure and to be strong for his sweetness. He had to be the strength she needed to pull through this. He had to be her rock…her "superman"…

CHAPTER 25

Tony

Tony held Korri's hand as she quietly slept in the hospital with machines beeping in time with her heartbeat. The doctors said she had a concussion and swelling around the wound. They put her in a medically induced coma to make sure there was no further swelling of her brain. The doctor informed Tony it would be another twenty-four hours of observation before Korrine would wake up; the process was slow, and some patients didn't wake up immediately. Tony didn't care how long it took; he wasn't leaving his sweetness until it was time to take her home.

A couple hours later, Brandon and Lauryn showed up to visit Korrine. Both were in tears and distraught over Korrine's condition. By the time the nurse came in to administer more pain meds, the pair had calmed somewhat.

"Is she going to wake up?" Brandon asked clearing his throat.

"Yes, the medicine is to help ease her out of the coma. The doctors didn't find any swelling of her brain; she just needs some rest. Ms. Taylor is going to be fine," the nurse replied with a small smile.

"Just push that button if you guys need anything," the nurse said as she left the room.

Brandon looked worried as he held Korri's free hand. He wiped the hair from her forehead and leaned in and kissed her cheek. He whispered words of love and said a small prayer before letting Lauryn take his place. He called a reluctant Tony away from Korri's bedside to have a conversation.

"You know, Korri doesn't have any immediate family, but we should call her cousin, Charlie. She and Korri were close growing up, and they still keep in touch. She lives in Houston, and I think she should be here," Brandon informed Tony.

"Yeah, we should definitely call her. But I'm not leaving Korri for even one minute. Please make the call and the arrangements for her to get here, and I will take care of the rest," Tony responded.

Brandon smiled. "You love her." It was a statement and not a question.

Tony responded with a small smile. "More than you could ever know."

****

Jake

"Hey, boss, our package has been delivered," Mike said to Jake as he ducked under the yellow crime-scene tape upon returning from the hospital.

"Great! That's one less thing I have to worry about. How's Korri?" Jake asked.

"Medically induced coma. Brandon and Lauryn just arrived when I left," Mike responded. "What about the other suspect? Do we let Tony know?"

"Not yet. He's dealing with enough. Langston is in the hands of the Feds, luckily for him," Jake sneered. "Everything is pretty much wrapped up here. I left Sanders and the boys just in case there's any need for any damage control, but we're pretty much in the clear. Let's go handle this package and give my cousin some peace. We have a lot of loose ends to tie up with all this mess. We still have to get down to Georgia and help with that whole mess, and I doubt for one second Tony will be leaving Korri anytime soon. So it's on me."

"Yeah, like you don't love all this shit," Mike chuckled. "This is right up your alley."

Jake laughed. "True, but you didn't have to say the shit out loud...damn chucklehead."

An hour later, Jake and Mike walked into an undisclosed location. Not many people even knew this place existed, but it came in handy to be ex-special forces. Both men sauntered into the building and were immediately greeted by a familiar face. Seth Young worked with Jake and Mike on the Special Forces team. But when Mike and Jake called it quits, Seth stayed in and now he's one of the head honchos. He's always a phone call away.

"Fellas, your package awaits in Room 2," Seth said while leading Mike and Jake to the room. "But you don't have much time. We have a delivery to the Feds before the end of the day, so make it quick."

Once in the room, the two men were greeted by a pair of wide brown eyes and a shocked expression.

"Misty?... Or is it Victoria now?" Jake stated simply. "You didn't think you could actually dye your hair and put in contacts and we wouldn't recognize you? We are professionals. We track people for a living, and we let you stay free. We knew your greed would lead us to Korri. We let you make it to the airport; we had to be sure you weren't meeting anybody else."

Tears started to slowly fall down Misty's face, as the realization hit that she was no longer a free woman. All her scheming and planning was for nothing. She no longer had to worry about family, love, or even money because she would be behind bars.

'H-how did you know it was me?" Misty stuttered. "I was so careful…"

"No, you weren't careful. We have a witness to the kidnapping, and Korri will be able to identify you," Jake said simply.

"I was supposed to be long gone with my new identity before she was even rescued," Misty said as the free flowing tears were now a distant memory.

"Misty, you were never going to get away with this...*never*...but maybe you can help yourself...What do you know about your father's shady dealings in Florida?"

A sinister smile spread across Misty's face. "I know enough that I want some sort of deal."

****

Korrine

Korrine woke from what seemed like a deep sleep. Her head no longer felt like it was going to explode, but it definitely felt like she had one helluva hangover. She slowly looked around the room and saw all the people she loved. Tony was lying with his head resting on top of her hand while Brandon and Lo were each scrunched up on a small couch in the corner of the room. She heard the beeping of the machines, and she could feel the wires connected to her. But this didn't look much like a hospital room; it looked more like a hotel room, and a nice one at that. She looked back down at the man she loved, and she knew for a fact that this man had everything to do with her accommodations. Korrine smiled lovingly as she ran a hand through his disheveled hair. She knew he would be worried and running his hands through it over and over again in frustration. As she gazed down at him, he slowly lifted his head and opened his eyes with a lazy smile forming on his lips. Yep, Korri was a goner. How could you not love those deep brown eyes and those sexy as sin dimples?

"There's my sweetness…I was worried about you, young lady," Tony said sitting up and kissing Korrine's hand.

"Hi, baby. Sorry you worried," Korrine replied shyly.

"No, baby. None of this is your fault, and I am truly sorry," Tony replied sadly. "This was about me or, more specifically, my money. Your involvement with me is the reason you were kidnapped. It had nothing to do with you. Sweetness, there's nothing I could do to make up for everything you've been through. However, this is something we can talk about later when you're out of this place."

"We can't control other people, baby. Those psychos were money hungry lunatics. There was no way to know what lengths they would go through to get money…." Korri said looking deeply into Tony's eyes.

"You're right, but you know I'm not letting you out of my sight for a while, right?" Tony stated seriously.

Korri smiled. "I figured as much."

Tony leaned down to kiss Korrine on her lips when he heard a screech coming from the doorway.

"You're awake!!!" Brandon yelled as he and Lo crossed the room in a rush to get to Korri's bed. "Baby girl, you scared the shit out of us! Don't you ever scare me like that again!"

Tony groaned as he barely got to brush his lips against hers. "You owe me a kiss."

Korrine laughed. "Ahhh, baby, I will give you so much more than that when I get out of here."

Tony groaned again, simultaneously releasing Korrine so Lo and Brandon could hug her.

"Korri, I'm so glad you're awake. I was so worried," Lo said with a bright smile, but with tears in her eyes.

"Oh, guys. I'm fine. I promise," Korrine replied hugging both her best friends.

While the friends were being reunited, the doctor walked in with a woman about Korrine's height. With milk chocolate skin, she had long braids down to the middle of her back and big hazel eyes like Korrine's.

"Charlie?!!"   Korrine   smiled   excitedly.
"How?…When?…You're here!…I'm so glad to see you!"

"Hey, baby girl." Charlie rushed to her bedside. Lo and Brandon gave her room to hug her cousin. "How in the hell did you get yourself kidnapped?" Charlie asked with a raised eyebrow.

"I'm sure that is a long and interesting story, but Ms. Taylor needs her rest," the doctor said addressing the room.

Grumbles were heard from each of the visitors, but they all bid Korrine a goodbye before heading towards the door…all except Tony, who refused to leave Korrine's side.

Korrine was finally able to talk Tony into stepping out to take the phone call from Jake, who had been calling all night. Jake let Tony know that everything had been wrapped up, and everyone involved with Korrine's kidnapping had been apprehended. Tony was livid when he found out Jeff was the one helping Misty, but he was glad that the FBI had the piece of shit because otherwise he would probably kill him with his bare hands. He couldn't believe the audacity of Misty and Jeff, and even his father, to get money from him. But taking Korrine was one mistake that he would personally see to it that they paid for.

****

Korrine was being released from the hospital after being there for almost a week and a half. It was precaution since they had to put her in a medically induced coma. Tony, of course, never left her side for more than a couple of hours. Korrine made him go and shower and get something to eat. She had to promise to do unspeakable things to get him to go, but it was worth it. Plus, as sexy as he is all rugged with a five o'clock shadow, he was starting to smell.

As Korrine and Tony were packing up what few things she had at the hospital, Charlie walked in.

"Hey, baby girl. I came to help you pack. How are you feeling today?" Charlie asked as she hugged Korri.

"I'm good, cousin. I'm really glad you came up here for me. It really means a lot," Korri replied hugging Charlie with all she had.

"Aw, Korri. We're all the family we have left. Of course, I would be here for you."

"I hate to break up this love fest, but I'm feeling a little left out here," Tony said with a fake pout.

"My bad, big guy," Charlie apologized with a smile. "You doing all right taking care of my cousin?"

Just when he was about to give a snarky reply, he heard a throat clearing. Jake was standing in the doorway, his arms crossed over his broad chest with a strange look on his face.

"Ah, Jake. How's it going, buddy?" Tony greeted with a knowing smirk.

"I'm good, buddy," Jake said, never breaking eye contact with Charlie. "I'll be even better when you introduce me to your new friend here."

"Oh, of course. Charlie, this lunkhead is my cousin Jake. Jake, this beautiful little lady here is Charlie, Korrine's cousin from Houston," Tony said looking between the two as if watching a tennis match.

Korrine cleared her throat, trying to get her cousin's attention.

Charlie looked at Korrine mouthing "dayum" as she turned to face Jake.

"Hi, I'm Charlene Heart," she told him as she extended her hand. "But everyone calls me Charlie."

"It's very nice to meet you, Ms. Heart." Jake was nearly breathless as he returned her handshake, realizing how good her skin felt against his. "I'm Jacob Cameron. As you see, everyone calls me Jake…"

"Well, I'm glad we are all getting...*familiar*...with one another," Korrine said, grabbing Tony's hand and moving towards the exit. "How about we blow this popsicle stand? I'm ready for some real food and a real shower."

EPILOGUE

Six Months Later

It had been a long couple of months after the kidnapping when Tony's father was indicted on fraud and conspiracy charges, and so was Gregory Austin. They turned state's evidence, but both men were still sentenced to fifteen years for all of the crimes they committed. Misty also helped with the evidence against her father and Anderson Cameron. But with the extra kidnapping, criminal assault, and conspiracy to commit fraud charges, she too was sentenced to fifteen years in prison. Jeff received ten years for the part he played, and Steve received seven years probation for his role, with an additional order of protection to stay away from Korrine. If the restraining order is ever violated, he will go to prison.

With most of the cases wrapped up and behind them, Korrine was able to get back to a sense of normalcy. In the days that followed, she had a body guard around the clock, which this time she didn't mind or fight. Although both Misty and Jeff were caught, she still felt scared sometimes. But she was getting through it with the support of her friends and her man.

Charlie decided to stay in town and help Korri get adjusted, and she was even thinking about relocating to Dallas. Korri started designing again and had a whole new clothing line worked out. She had new clients, and she was putting the past behind her.

Tony stuck his head into Korrine's bedroom. "Baby, we're going to be late for dinner." "I'm coming, baby. I was just looking for my other earring..." Korrine stopped talking once she noticed the look on Tony's face.

"What's wrong, superman? You okay?" Korri asked at the concerned look on Tony's face.

Tony stalked closer to Korri as if she were his prey. "I uh-uh...damn, baby...we're definitely going to be late..."

"Babe," Korri giggled, pushing past Tony. "Baby, we gotta go."

"Yeah, but, sweetness, you're wearing my favorite red dress and you look so damn delicious. How am I supposed to concentrate when you look so delectable?"

Korri laughed as she slipped past Tony. "Antonio Cameron, what exactly do you need to concentrate on...?" Korri voice died off when she turned around and saw Tony down on one knee.

"Korrine Marie Taylor...I never thought I wanted love until I found you...I can't imagine my life without you...Sweetness, you are my entire world, and it would give me great pleasure if you did me the honor of becoming my wife."

Korri had tears rolling down her face and she let out a breath she hadn't known she was holding. She ran and wrapped her arms around Tony's neck sobbing like a child.

"Sweetness, is that a yes?"

"Yes! Baby, yes, I will be your wife!" Korri shrieked with tear soaked cheeks and laughter.

Korri and Tony were indeed late for dinner, but nobody cared when they shared their news upon their arrival.

As she showed off her ring, Korrine clung to her superman with the most blissful smile on her face.

The once shy designer had gotten everything she desired and more.

The End

ABOUT THE AUTHOR: I am a wife, daughter, sister, and educator. I've always had a love for reading, which turned into a love for writing as well. I wrote my first book purely as a stress reliever. I had a few friends read what I wrote and they liked it, so I finished the book. I never thought I would have the opportunity to become a published author, and I am both blessed and thankful! I look forward to others coming into my imagination and hopefully they enjoy it as much as I do!

PLEASE LEAVE ME ANY FEEDBACK! I WOULD LOVE TO HEAR FROM YOU! THANK YOU FOR READING, AND I HOPED YOU ENJOYED MY WORK.

KASEY_MARTIN79@YAHOO.COM
FACEBOOK.COM/KASEYMARTIN36